The killing of Jess Flemming, a minor-league hoodlum, brings Dr. Paul Standish, a physician who doubles as the city medical examiner, into an affair that implicates some prominent members of the community. To Police Lieutenant Ballard the case is cut and dried. The obvious suspect is Ralph Estey, a jazz trumpeter who has disappeared. But a second murder alters the situation markedly. Standish, compelled by a desire to learn the truth, not only as a medical examiner but as a man, conducts his own investigation. His inquiry into an accidental death of the previous year, in which Flemming ran his car over a well-known businessman, puts his own life in jeopardy before he is able to piece together the puzzle, which includes some entangled family finances and a surprising love affair.

Once again George Harmon Coxe has written a well-plotted, suspenseful story that tests the reader's faculties to the end.

Books by GEORGE HARMON COXE

Murder with Pictures (1935)

The Barotique Mystery (1936)   *The Camera Clue (1937)*

Four Frightened Women (1939)

Murder for the Asking (1939)   *The Glass Triangle (1939)*

The Lady Is Afraid (1940)   *No Time to Kill (1941)*

Mrs. Murdock Takes a Case (1941)

Silent Are the Dead (1942)   *Assignment in Guiana (1942)*

The Charred Witness (1942)

Alias the Dead (1943)   *Murder for Two (1943)*

Murder in Havana (1943)   *The Groom Lay Dead (1944)*

The Jade Venus (1945)

Woman at Bay (1945)   *Dangerous Legacy (1946)*

The Fifth Key (1947)   *Fashioned for Murder (1947)*

Venturous Lady (1948)

The Hollow Needle (1948)   *Lady Killer (1949)*

Inland Passage (1949)   *Eye Witness (1950)*

The Frightened Fiancée (1950)   *The Widow Had a Gun (1951)*

The Man Who Died Twice (1951)

Never Bet Your Life (1952)   *The Crimson Clue (1953)*

Uninvited Guest (1953)   *Focus on Murder (1954)*

Death at the Isthmus (1954)   *Top Assignment (1955)*

Suddenly a Widow (1956)   *Man on a Rope (1956)*

Murder on Their Minds (1957)

One Minute Past Eight (1957)   *The Impetuous Mistress (1958)*

The Big Gamble (1958)   *Slack Tide (1959)*

Triple Exposure (1959) CONTAINING

The Glass Triangle, The Jade Venus, & The Fifth Key

One Way Out (1960)   *The Last Commandment (1960)*

Error of Judgment (1961)   *Moment of Violence (1961)*

The Man Who Died Too Soon (1962)   *Mission of Fear (1962)*

The Hidden Key (1963)   *One Hour to Kill (1963)*

Deadly Image (1964)   *With Intent to Kill (1965)*

The Reluctant Heiress (1965)   *The Ring of Truth (1966)*

THE
RING OF
TRUTH

GEORGE HARMON COXE

LONDON

HAMMOND HAMMOND COMPANY

First published in Great Britain 1967
© Copyright 1966 George Harmon Coxe

FOR CAROL

BR/BR

Printed in Great Britain by
Lowe & Brydone (Printers) Ltd., for
Hammond, Hammond & Co. Ltd.
2 Clement's Inn, London, W.C.2
1·67

I

TO CERTAIN HABITUES, Hennessey's was known primarily as a restaurant, even though the food service was limited to dinner. Others, more concerned with drink and entertainment, looked upon the establishment as a nightclub because of the music which was offered after nine o'clock, and the tiny dance floor for odd couples who could not resist the driving beat of Ralph Estey's five-piece band.

On this particular Friday night in late April, Dr. Paul Standish belonged to the second category. He had been a fan of Estey's since he had heard him blowing his trumpet as a sideman at Nick's in New York's Greenwich Village when he himself was serving his first year of internship in one of the city's hospitals. In the past year or more that Estey's group had been established at Hennessey's, Standish had stopped in on the average of once a week, sometimes to have dinner, sometimes to listen, sometimes with Mary Hayward, who was his nurse, secretary, and girl Friday, but more often alone for a drink while Estey played a set or two of his solid Dixieland music.

Now, having paid his check during the last intermission, he was about to leave when he became aware of some commotion behind him. His small table was not far from the entrance foyer and checkroom, and what he heard first was a woman's voice that sounded shrill, alarmed, and furious. Turning at once, he saw the street door closing and knew that the cry had come from the sidewalk outside.

"Stop!" That was what he heard first. "Stop it, I tell you!"

He was on his feet as the door closed off the sound and, stepping round the slatted partition, aware that two other men had risen and were moving behind him, he noticed that Sheila Keith was not in her accustomed place behind the checkroom counter.

He saw her as he opened the outer door. She was standing beside the uniformed doorman, who seemed to be restraining her. A big, bareheaded man who seemed vaguely familiar was standing on the sidewalk, hands on hips, his head outthrust and slightly bent. Stretched out in front of him, on his back with his head on the curb, was Ralph Estey.

For another second or two no one moved. The immediate conclusion that came to Standish was an obvious one, but it was as a doctor that he stepped to Estey's side and went to one knee. Behind him he could hear Sheila Keith saying: "Oh, damn you, Jess Flemming! Damn you!"

In the next moment the trumpet player's head moved. He raised it a few inches, the eyes opening. As he struggled to sit up, Standish helped him but prevented him from rising.

"Take it easy, Ralph. Easy boy. What happened?"

"I got clipped," Estey said with some bewilderment.

"Jess slugged him," Sheila Keith snapped, and glared at the big man.

"He swung first," Flemming said.

"Ralph hit his head when he fell," the girl said, her voice bitter and contemptuous.

"I'm all right," Estey said, still struggling to rise.

"Stay put!" Standish ordered. "Let me look."

He took out his pencil flashlight and examined the back of Estey's head, noting the abrasion beneath the thinning hair, the incipient swelling. He glanced up, addressing no one in particular.

"How long was he out?"

"Ten, twelve seconds maybe," the doorman said.

Standish shifted the flashlight to bring the beam on Estey's face. He noted the bruise on the cheekbone and, over the other's protest, examined first one eye and then the other to see the reaction of the pupils.

Estey wrenched his head away and spoke irritably. "Look, Doc, I'm all right." Again he tried to rise. This time Standish helped him and spoke severely.

"You've had a concussion, and concussions are tricky things. As your doctor"—Standish had treated him professionally for a touch of virus some months ago—"I'd advise you to go to the hospital. I can run you over there in—"

"No."

"Spend the night. Just for observation. If there should be a delayed reaction—and there often is—we can take some X rays—"

Estey's objection was softly profane and then, his voice suddenly hard and vicious, he addressed Jess Flemming.

"Okay, Jess. Tonight I moved out of my class but what I said still goes. Keep bothering Sheila and I'll call you again. Only next time I'll be carrying a gun. Put your hands on me just once and I'll kill you."

"Sure." Flemming grunted derisively. "Carry your gun, little man. Just stay out of my way."

Sheila Keith watched him open the door and step inside, her young face tight and her eyes stormy. She seemed about to call after him, then turned to Estey.

"I'm sorry, Ralph. You shouldn't have bothered him. I told you what he was like." She stepped close and put her fingers against his cheek. "Does it hurt?"

"No." Estey pulled his face away. "I'm all right, I tell you. Look, Doc—"

But Standish was no longer listening. A third man had joined the group while he had been occupied with Estey, a slender well-dressed fellow with metal-rimmed spectacles. The shadowed face seemed familiar but when he could not place it he addressed the two men who, like himself, had stepped outside to see what was happening. He did not know them but it did not matter and he spoke with authority.

"I'm a doctor," he said. "I want a better look at him. Help him into the men's room and keep him there. I'll be with you in two minutes."

He turned then, ignoring Estey's muttered protests, and crossed the street diagonally to the parking lot where he'd left his car. When he had unlocked it, he took out his doctor's bag and recrossed the street.

The two strangers were standing just inside the doorway to the men's room when Standish entered. The attendant, a stooped and ancient Negro, was watching Estey as he stood before the mirror examining the bruise on his cheekbone.

"If I slap a little powder on it," he said reaching for a can of talcum, "you'll never notice it."

"Take off your coat, Ralph," Standish said. "Roll up your sleeve."

Estey lowered his hands and turned. He drew a visible and elaborate breath and seemed about to protest. His dark eyes had a truculent look but Standish stared him down, standing perfectly still and saying nothing until the breath was expelled noisily and Estey started to peel off his jacket.

There was a single wooden chair in the room and Standish motioned Estey toward it as he opened his bag and took out his blood-pressure apparatus.

Estey eyed it with distaste. "What the hell is that?"

"If you want the proper name, a sphygmomanometer."

"To take my blood pressure?"

"Right."

When Standish had taken Estey's pulse and found it strong and somewhat rapid, he wrapped the expanding cuff around the bare arm and pumped air with the rubber bulb, pumped again. He read the scale and released the pressure.

"What's it say?" Estey asked.

"One seventy-eight over eighty-two."

"How's that stack up?"

"How old are you?"

"Forty the next time around."

"A little high."

Standish replaced the apparatus and reached for his ophthalmoscope. He told Estey to look at a certain spot across the room and snapped on the light beam, leaning close as he examined first one eye and then the other. He saw nothing particularly alarming but when Estey started to rise he pushed him back, holding him there with one hand on top of his head while he reached for his otoscope.

"What are you doing?" Estey demanded.

"I'm going to put this in your ear. Hold still. . . . I'm also," he added when he had examined both ears, "going to put a light up your nose. Tip your head back."

Estey did so, grumbling. Finally he said: "What the hell are you trying to prove?"

"That you don't show any outward signs of a fracture."

"Would I still be conscious if I did?"

"You might. What I'm looking for is any sign of blood or cerebral spinal fluid." He straightened. "Luckily I don't see any. I still think it would be wise to—"

"Sure." Estey rolled down his sleeve as Standish began to repack his bag. "But it's like I told you, Doc. I'm okay. A little headache maybe but a good belt of booze will fix that. Also"—he put on his jacket—"I've got to get the next set started. One thing that bastard Flemming could have done and didn't. If he'd slugged me in the mouth and split a lip I'd be out of a job for a month."

He combed his thinning hair and adjusted his tie, a frail-looking man with a long bony face and prominent ears. A small eyebrow-width mustache contrasted strikingly with the grayish indoor complexion, and when he stood erect his torso had a flat-chested, almost concave look that made Standish wonder where he got the lung capacity to blow a horn the way he did. Now, turning from the mirror, he grinned and tapped the doctor's shoulder.

"Thanks," he said. "Stick around and I'll buy you a drink."

As Standish followed Estey out and turned toward the foyer, he decided he could have another drink and listen to one more set. It was not because of Estey's suggestion, which he understood was not really an invitation as much as something to say. But it was Friday night and, barring some emergency calls, tomorrow should be an easy day. This is what he told himself but in the back of his mind and not yet admitted for argument was the thought that he wanted one more look at Estey's eyes after a strenuous half hour of blowing the trumpet.

At the checkroom he put his doctor's bag on the counter, giving Sheila Keith a moment of quick inspection as he asked her to put it with his coat. No more than average height, she had a trim and well-proportioned figure, with a nicely defined bust and shapely legs, the noticeable firmness of the calves suggesting that she had done some dancing. Above the demure but snug-fitting dark-gray dress with the white collar her hair was ash-blond and looked natural. The eyes were greenish, the brows upward-slanting to lend a look of sexiness to her face. Her mouth was small but lipstick helped it and her chin was determined except when she smiled.

In her line of work this was often, for she had learned the value of the proper approach. She had a mildly flirtatious air which seemed guileless but was in fact studied and part of her act. When she said good evening, when she took your coat or held it, there was a look of intimacy in the eyes and the curve of her mouth that promised something. She made you feel it. You knew somehow that you would never get this promised reward but it was nice to contemplate and made the quarter tipper put a half dollar in the tray more often than not. But at the moment the smile was forced and she wasn't trying very hard.

"Is he all right?"

"I think so," Standish said. "I want another look at his eyes after the next set but I don't believe there's anything to worry about. Did Flemming leave?"

"Any moment now." She gave a small jerk of her head. "He's having some words with Mr. Hennessey."

Estey had tapped his group into a chorus of "Back Home in Indiana," and as Standish stepped back he saw Jess Flemming at the near corner of the bar. Standing close was Hennessey, a short but stocky man in his fifties with a pink face and not much hair. Across the bar but leaning over it was the head barman, a tall and beefy man named Larry. Standish, deciding against a table this time, moved behind the trio. They took no notice of him as he slid upon the next stool, and though they kept their voices down he heard the end of the conversation.

"I've warned you before, Flemming," Hennessey was saying. "This time I mean it. Stay out of here. Don't come in again."

Flemming looked down at Hennessey, a tall, well-built man of forty or so with a paunch that was beginning to show. He was a flashy dresser, big-boned and not bad-looking in a coarse-featured way, but there was also an inbred streak of meanness that showed in the hard pale eyes and the twist of his mouth.

"It's a public place."

"And I reserve the right," Hennessey said softly, "to keep objectionable people out. You're objectionable, on all counts."

"If I come in, you call the cops, is that it?"

"You come in and we'll escort you out."

"Who's we?"

"Me and Larry. Now beat it."

Flemming took a long look at Larry, who eyed him calmly, straightened, and said nothing. Flemming gave a tug at his jacket, started to turn away, stopped for a final comment.

"I might try it sometime. Between the three of us we might break up the joint."

"I'm insured," Hennessey said. "And I understand the mob won't be backing you any more. It'll be just you and us."

Hennessey turned away and so did Flemming. Larry seemed to notice Standish for the first time. "Oh hello, Doctor," he said. "Scotch and water? Ralph okay?"

Standish said Ralph was fine. When he had his drink he turned his back to the bar and glanced over the room. It was still well filled and his idle glance focused finally on a table he had noticed earlier. There had been two people there at the time. Now there were three and, not meaning to, his mind went back to a Saturday night four months before. The recent presence of Jess Flemming became at once a part of the picture, and the element of coincidence, at first nebulous and without definition, became stronger as he let his thoughts move on.

For Standish wore two hats. With one he was a young doctor with a modest but growing private practice; with the other he was the medical examiner, in a city of this size not a full-time job nor, for him, a permanent one. And it had been as medical examiner that he had investigated a traffic death that occurred on the street outside around the middle of December.

His attention still on the table, he identified the woman as Evelyn Tremaine, the widow of the man who had been run down and killed. She was a striking-looking brunette in her early thirties, smartly dressed in her navy suit. Her companion, Warren Choate, had been Robert Tremaine's partner in a small brokerage house and Standish had heard that Choate was presently separated from his wife.

They had been at the same table when Standish arrived and he assumed that they had dined here and stayed on to do a little drinking while they listened to Ralph Estey's group. The third member of the trio had apparently

stopped in recently for a drink, a slender, bespectacled
man named Donald Tremaine, the younger brother of the
dead man. Now, taking a second look, Standish identified
him as the man who had appeared on the sidewalk while
he had been administering to the fallen Estey.

The element of coincidence that began to occupy the doctor's thoughts came from the fact that the Tremaines and
the Choates had spent the evening here on that fatal December night. The Choates had left earlier—Standish could
not remember why—and the Tremaines were among the
last to go. Robert Tremaine, as was his Saturday-night custom, was drunk. He had needed some help with his coat
and getting out the door. Spurning the assistance of the
doorman, he had started across the street toward the parking lot with his wife trying to support him. As he moved out
between the parked cars, a sedan accelerating from a short
distance down the street struck him before the driver could
stop.

The driver of that car was Jess Flemming, and it was
Dr. Standish's testimony that kept him from being charged
with vehicular homicide.

There had been a light snow earlier which had melted
and left the pavements slick. Flemming had had one
whiskey with a beer chaser at a workingman's tavern down
the street, and a quick blood test showed a negligible alcohol content. A prompt autopsy on Robert Tremaine sub-
stantiated the story of the witnesses, since the blood alcohol
test was far above the legal maximum denoting drunk-
enness.

The condition of the street, the darkness, the fact that
Flemming had just started up and was still in second gear,
were factors at the hearing, but the doctor's testimony and
the doorman's story were sufficiently conclusive to absolve
the driver. Flemming's traffic record showed three convictions over a period of years, but with the absence of negligence or criminal intent the case became one for traffic

court. Flemming was found guilty of reckless driving and a technical charge of "driving to endanger." He had been fined one hundred dollars, with his license suspended for sixty days. . . .

Standish's thoughts reverted to the moment when he realized that the three people were on their feet and about to leave. He also was aware that the music had stopped and the bandstand was empty. When he could not locate Estey and was sure he was not table hopping, he finished his drink and went looking for him.

2

THERE WERE two doorways leading to the rear area of Hennessey's, one on either side of the bandstand. On the right, double swinging doors with glass inserts led directly to the kitchen; on the left, a curtained doorway gave on a hall with Hennessey's private entrance on the ground floor and, just ahead of it, were stairs leading to two rooms above.

Over the years the entertainment policy of the establishment had changed from more elaborate cabaret-type acts to the simple presentation of a working band. There had been a need at one time for dressing rooms and the first of these, the smaller of the two, was now the personal province of the musicians, a hideout between sets for card games and private drinking for those not inclined to mingle with the patrons or unwilling to listen to a lot of silly chatter as the price of a drink.

A cleaning woman swept out once a week, usually Mondays; the rest of the time the men policed the room themselves. No one was allowed inside except by invitation, including Hennessey himself, and such guests were usually

limited to the members of the profession—agents, song
pluggers, arrangers, itinerant musicians less lucky at the moment than themselves, and, sometimes, girls.

Standish knew all this. He also was aware of the clannish
snobbery of the breed. He had seen it demonstrated in other
places. If there was a musicians' table and some enthusiastic
buff joined it unasked between sets, there would be a grad-
ual one-by-one exodus until the final member of the band
excused himself and stood up. Only then did the outsider
realize how openly he had been snubbed and abandoned,
and by that time he had no choice but to slink back to his
own table and companions, feeling like a pariah who had
been publicly exposed. That is why Standish knocked at the
closed door and stood patiently until Ralph Estey opened it.

Over the trumpet man's shoulders Standish could see the
interior with its threadbare carpet and discarded furniture.
The piano player was stretched out on a battered-looking
studio couch. The drummer and trombone player were
playing gin rummy across an oblong table, and the clarinet
man who doubled on the sax was slouched in the room's one
easy chair with a copy of *Variety*. Estey's pale thin face
wore a practiced frown until he recognized his visitor. The
look of surprise that followed seemed genuine.

"Oh," he said, as though he had not seen Standish in three
weeks.

"You said something about buying a drink."

"Yeah," Estey said uncertainly. "That's right, I did."

"Then let's go downstairs," Standish said. "That way I
won't have to invade your sanctuary."

By that time he had Estey by the arm and there was no
further protest as they went down the stairs and past the
bandstand and found a table off in one corner.

A waiter moved up and asked Estey if he would have the
usual. Estey said no, he'd have brandy with a spot of soda
on the side. Standish, not wanting a drink but aware that he
had to continue the pretense, asked for another Scotch and

water. When the waiter went away, he reached for Estey's wrist.

"Hold still," he said when Estey tried to pull away.

"I'm all right," Estey said, but he made no further move and after ten seconds Standish removed his fingers.

"I'm beginning to believe you're right. How's the headache?"

"About gone."

"So what was that all about outside? Did you really swing at Flemming first?"

"Hell yes."

"Why?"

"Because he was bothering Sheila."

"In what way?"

"Oh"—Estey gestured impatiently—"hanging around and wanting to take her home and calling her up."

"He's a very mean guy from what I hear."

"Sure. But I wasn't thinking about that. I was sore. We had some words and he asked me if I wanted to step outside and repeat them, so I did."

Standish considered the statement and was impressed. It made him wonder if perhaps Estey had more courage than good sense. Then he remembered something else.

"Have you really got a gun?"

"Sure. An old H & R .32. I've had it for years."

"And if he roughs you up again you're going to use it?"

"Damn right."

Standish grunted softly. "Oh, great," he said. "That would take care of Flemming all right. These days you probably wouldn't get the chair either. What would probably happen is that you'd wind up leading the prison band for the next thirty years."

"Not me." Estey shook his head and there was a strange determination in his voice. "If I decide to kill him, I'll grab my horn and run for it. If I can't make it, I'll stick the gun in my mouth and pull the trigger. It would be a break for

Sheila and who the hell would care. I'm not going anywhere any more; I've been."

The waiter brought the drinks and Estey took a sip of brandy, a swallow of soda. He was scowling now and making little circles with the bottom of the brandy glass. Standish, watching him and bothered by what he had heard, spoke again of Jess Flemming.

"How long has Sheila known him?"

"Last year. Down in Florida. I was down there for a while. That's where I met her. Four of us were down there playing in a trap in Miami—not Miami Beach, Miami. She was doing some singing then and the boss put her on for a couple of weeks."

"She sang when she first came here, didn't she?"

"Right. Pretty good too. The trouble is there are a thousand other chicks in the same boat. Even if a girl has something special she needs a lot of breaks to make it big. She has to know the right people, and get the right agent to handle her, and have the right arrangements, and the right kind of promotion."

He took another sip of brandy and said: "I knew I had this spot lined up, so I asked her if she didn't want to come North and she said maybe if she knew she had a job. I talked Hennessey into giving her a two-week trial and she came."

"I heard her once, I think," Standish said. "She sounded pretty good to me."

"She was good enough but she's a smart kid and she knew the score. She's got a lot of determination and she knows what she wants. . . . You remember Jenny, the hat-check girl who was here before?"

"She got married."

"Right. When Sheila found out about it and got an idea of what Jenny was making, she thought she could do even better if she put on the right kind of act. She asked Hennessey for the job, figuring she wouldn't last as a singer, and he gave her a trial run. Well, she's got a good memory for faces, so that after once or twice you don't have to take a check, she'll remember you. She fusses over you just enough and gives you that smile that says you're really something special and the tips get bigger. Hell, she's making as much money now as I am, maybe more."

"How is it between you?"

"What do you mean?" Estey's glance came up, his head tipping slightly.

"Are you in love with her?"

"Maybe. I guess you'd call it that."

"And how does she feel?"

"She likes me okay, but if you mean is she going to marry me, I doubt it. Why the hell should she?"

"You're one of the best."

"Ha!"

Standish let the remark go and digressed.

"Your wife got the divorce?"

"Six months ago."

"Alimony?"

"No, thank God. Ruth had a new husband lined up. I send her twenty-five a week for the support of the boy—he's five now—and I had to take out an insurance policy for ten grand payable to him before she'd go for the divorce. No," he said, his thoughts coming back to the previous subject. "Sheila wants something better than a broken-down trumpet player. She wants a house in a suburb and kids and security—and who can blame her?"

He drained the last of the brandy from the glass and swallowed some soda. He slipped down in his chair, making his chest even more concave, and his gaze went beyond Standish to fix on something that only he could see.

"Things used to be different," he said, his voice softly reminiscent. "I remember when I went down to New York, just a kid out of high school. There were a dozen places then on Fifty-second Street, all of them jumping. Downtown there was Condon's and Nick's. You remember Nick's?"

"That's where I caught you for the first time."

"A real right guy, Nick," Estey said as though he had not heard. "He loved musicians, especially Dixieland musicians. You remember how he had that second piano down on the floor? When he felt like it he'd sit down and play along with the group, and enjoy every minute of it. So the poor guy died and pretty soon they closed the joint. The Embers is gone. The Roundtable changed to belly dancers. I don't know what they play there now but it ain't jazz. There's practically nothing on Fifty-second Street. So what you've got is Condon's and Jimmy Ryan's and the Metropole —if you want to stand up and blow your brains out."

He sighed, but the distance was still in his eyes. "The guys—real good guys—are standing in line to get into Condon's. They call up, or their wives do, once a week to see if there's going to be a change so they can bring a group in." He sighed again and now he looked at Standish. "Why do you think I'm up here in the sticks? I'll tell you. It's a job, and it's steady, and by giving these so-called jazz concerts Sunday afternoons around the state I pick up a little extra loot. That is, if we get a good-enough turnout.

"I'm not blaming anybody, you understand? There are a lot of good horn men around—Ruby Braff, Clark Terry, Don Jacoby, Howard McGhee—and they're cutting records and getting heard. I had my chances if I had been smart enough to grab them. I've done the big-band route. I played with most of the good ones. I had a couple of chances to snag on with a studio band years ago and if I had I'd be making three times the dough I'm getting now and I'd be getting it regularly. But no, I wanted to play my way."

He half turned in his chair, put one arm straight up until he caught the waiter's eye, and gave a pantomimic signal for another drink.

"What I didn't know then," he said, "is that it takes more than talent and hard work to make it big. You need some breaks. You need exposure and a genius for an agent. Take Al Hirt. A great Dixieland man, right? Fine technique."

"Sure."

"Ha! You're not even half right. Hirt played first trumpet with guys like Tommy and Jimmy Dorsey and Horace Heidt. Strictly big band. He didn't play jazz, he didn't improvise, he read what they put in front of him. But his home was in New Orleans and he had a wife and a couple of kids —he's got a flock of them now—and his wife wanted him home. Hell, he couldn't even play Dixieland. He had a staff job on a local radio station. And on the side he played two or three nights a week with a Dixieland group on Bourbon Street. At first he had to learn his parts and play them from memory while all the rest of them were improvising their heads off."

He watched the waiter place the drink in front of him and took a sip. "So he finally picked up enough Dixieland stuff to start his own combo. He worked Bourbon Street for three or four years until an agent heard him and wanted to sign him up. By then he had more kids and his wife said no, not unless he got more dough than anyone was about to offer for some unknown Dixieland band. So what happens? The agent gets him a´spot in Las Vegas. He plays there a month. Dinah Shore hears him and gives him a spot on her TV show. He gets another spot in New York. He gets a little more TV exposure through Dinah and Ed Sullivan. You know the rest of it. He gets a thirteen-week network TV show as a summer replacement. Sure he can play Dixieland now. He's got a good group with him. That little reed man and Freddie Crane, his piano player—great. Hirt's getting the loot but he's a pop trumpet player, he'll tell you so himself."

He took another swallow of his drink and said: "What about Pete Fountain? I understand he played for Hirt after Hirt went Dixieland. So how does Fountain make it? By sticking it out two years with Lawrence Welk. He takes a solo a week and millions of people see him and then he comes back to New Orleans and there it only takes a few thousand to open up a club."

"You made a lot of records," Standish said. "I've got some of them."

"Yeah. I've made a million of them. But I never gave the downbeat. I didn't have enough brains or push or a good-enough agent to front for a band. I'd cut out a record and take my dough and stick my horn under my arm and that was that." He leaned forward, tapping the table top with his index finger for emphasis, his remoteness gone and the sound of reality in his voice.

"I've got some damn good boys with me right now. Do you know what they get? Scale. There's some guys around that get less than that."

"But," Standish said, his surprise showing, "how can that be? If they belong to the union—and they have to, don't they?—they have to be paid the union scale."

Estey said "Ha!" again and his laugh was abrupt and mirthless.

"Oh, they get it on paper all right. That's how their checks are made out, and that's how the owners put it down on their income tax, but if you're real hard up and you need the work—and don't think the bosses don't know the score—you'll kick back twenty bucks a week under the table if you have to. And you know why things are so tough?" he demanded.

"Why?" said Standish, coming in on cue.

"Rock-and-roll. These screwy dances the society guys and gals are going for. You know what they have now in real swish joints that used to have bands and a reputation? Record players, maybe backed up with a band consisting of three guitars, a bass, and a mechanical drummer. Guitars," he said, making the word profane. "I hope I never see one again, unless maybe George Van Epps or Charlie Byrd is holding it. What the hell is the name of this new craze everybody's got—discotheques. French, isn't it? You know what it means?"

"Not exactly."

"Me either. To me it means no bands, no live musicians. They got a couple in town and they don't even *have* a band: just records. Look at this combo of mine. Solid, but where's my bass player? Hennessey won't go for the extra salary. 'You sound okay without one,' he says. Ha!"

"He's right about your sounding great," Standish said, "but I guess it means you have to work a little harder or blow a little louder or something."

"You said it." Estey pulled himself erect in his chair and grinned. "So why should a smart, ambitious, good-looking chick like Sheila settle for a guy like me?"

"You're selling yourself a little short, aren't you?"

"Not permanently, I hope."

"If you both work for a while—"

"No." Estey shook his head. "That's no good. But don't get the idea I'm giving up, Doc. I've got some things lined up that don't look too bad. Maybe next year—"

He broke off as a chord sounded on the piano and he turned quickly to find the piano player seated and the other three men moving onto the bandstand. He pushed back his chair and came to his feet.

"I got to go," he said, glancing at his watch as he did so. "If I don't start blowing I'll have Hennessey on my tail. See you, Doc. I didn't mean to run off at the mouth like that."

Standish left his unfinished drink and signaled the waiter for the check that he had not expected Estey to pay. When he had added a tip and signed it, he started for the doorway. Apparently Sheila Keith had seen him coming—she made it a point of being alert for departing guests she knew, especially good tippers—because she had his hat in one hand, his coat over her arm. Her smile was much better now, the veiled intimacy, which Standish understood was deliberate, working in her greenish eyes.

"You had quite a session with Ralph," she said as she held his coat. "You're sure he's all right now?"

"As sure as I can be."

"I never saw him so angry. He's not like that usually."

"I guess he had all he could take from Flemming. A man who is jealous enough—"

"Jealous?" The shadowed eyes opened. "Of me? He had no reason to be." She put his doctor's bag on the counter while Standish produced a half dollar. "What did he say? He was kidding about the gun, wasn't he?"

Standish adjusted his collar. "He says he has one and if he takes you home tonight—"

"Oh, he doesn't take me home. I mean, not often."

"But you're good friends?"

"Oh, yes. I think he's wonderful. He got me my job."

"But not enough to marry him."

"Is that what he said?"

Standish grinned at her. "I'm not sure I remember exactly what he did say. Maybe you should ask him. If you get a chance, tell him not to get silly about the gun. That bit on the sidewalk was probably just talk. He'll be okay once he calms down."

"Sure he will." The smile came back, bright and approving. "Good night, Doctor."

3

UNTIL 9:50 in the evening of the following Monday, Paul Standish had devoted his time, as a young doctor should, to the demands of his growing private practice. Monday was one of his clinic days and he had spent most of the morning in the hospital. Office patients scheduled between one and three had been more numerous than usual, and Mary Hayward, on her own initiative, had made appointments for three workingmen between six and seven.

Standish had dined quietly and alone at the University Club and he was looking forward to some reading and an early bedtime when he put his car away in the row of garages that flanked the alley in back of his apartment. He came out on the street, swung right at the next corner, and not until he approached the entrance of his apartment house was it necessary for him to put on his second hat and face up to the additional duties of his official job as medical examiner.

The deduction was a simple one, once he spotted the police sedan at the curb and recognized the driver. It had happened before, and he knew that the dispatcher at Headquarters had been trying to reach him and, failing in this, had sent the driver to wait for him. He stepped into the car resignedly, aware that his reading would have to be postponed and that he would not get to bed until the job was done—whenever that happened to be.

"What is it this time?" he asked as the driver put the car in gear.

"A shooting. Homicide, I guess."

They drove rapidly crosstown, coming presently to this block on the outer fringe of the downtown section, a neighborhood of small, discouraged-looking shops and low-rent apartment houses. The driver got as close as he could to the entrance of a three-story building, its original beige-brick façade now soot-stained and depressing in the darkness. Lights shone from most of the front windows, and heads were silhouetted there as the neighbors peered out to watch the activity on the sidewalk below. Two police cars were angled into the curb opposite the entrance, an ambulance was double-parked, and a uniformed officer kept traffic moving.

Standish spoke to the ambulance driver, and the police-
man at the street door saluted and said: "Third floor, Doc."

Television sounds came from behind closed doors as he
climbed the narrow, rubber-treaded stairs to the third floor,
where one of the two facing doors stood open. The living
room he entered was hot, stuffy, and crowded, but only the
police photographer, who was still busy, paid any attention
to the still figure in the easy chair.

The senior officer present was a hard-jawed, hairy-eared
veteran named Captain Cavanaugh. An experienced and
competent professional, he was the city's Chief of Detectives and in line for the top job. Next to him stood Lieutenant Ballard of the Homicide Squad, a term which was
something of a joke since the Homicide Squad consisted of
Ballard, a sergeant named Cooney, and a clerk-stenog-
rapher, who could be called upon when needed. The investigation of homicide was Ballard's province and he was
head man, but in practice every detective in the depart-
ment pitched in when needed.

Cavanaugh had a dead cigar in one corner of his mouth,
his hat pushed back. There was no animosity between him
and Standish but the captain had made it plain that he did
not entirely approve of the medical-examiner law, particularly the part which said that a body could not be moved
until official permission was given. In addition there had
been at least one case when Standish's post-mortem findings
had complicated what had originally seemed like a simple
case of homicide. Now, his impatience showing, he said:

"Where were you, Doc? We've been dragging our feet."

Standish glanced at Ballard, who gave him a small wink.
He put down his bag and unbuttoned his topcoat. "Not
long, I hope," he said.

The room, what he could see of it, was more expensively
furnished than he had expected from the outward appearance of the building and the neighborhood. The divan on
which he put his coat and hat was long and heavy, the color

television set was a console model, and the plain-colored rug was soft underfoot. He did not stop to wonder about this at the moment. Nor was there any thought in his mind that the element of coincidence he had considered on Friday night at Hennessey's was still at work.

For the man in the chair, clad now in slacks, loafers, and a yellow sport shirt darkly stained in front, was Jess Flemming. Even though the head was tipped forward Standish had recognized him the instant he entered the room and now, approaching the chair, he could not help remembering the scene outside Hennessey's and Ralph Estey's threat. He could not obliterate the thought and he did not know what he was going to do about it. Because it was too disturbing to contemplate, he pushed it far back in his brain and gave his attention to the job at hand.

"Who found him? How did you find out about it? Someone hear the shot?"

"Not that we know of," Ballard said. "We got a quick rundown on the other tenants—those that were home—and every damn one of them had the TV on. They say that's all they heard."

"A phone call," Cavanaugh added. "To Headquarters." He grunted disgustedly. "The guy on the switchboard can't say if it was a man, woman, or child, only that the voice was kind of husky. Said there had been some trouble in apartment 3-B at this address and we ought to send a cop."

Standish leaned over the body, which had slumped backward, one leg bent, the other outthrust. He took the head in his hands and turned it, testing the neck for *rigor*. He did the same with the hands and the wrists, the elbows, the knees. He opened the shirt, noting a small round hole just to the left of center. He slid one hand up under the armpit to get some idea of body heat, examined first one eye and then the other.

"How long?" Cavanaugh asked.

"I'd say not less than an hour—which you probably already know—and not more than two. I doubt if I can put it any closer after the p.m."

"Yeah." Cavanaugh swiveled the dead cigar to the other corner of his mouth and readjusted his hat. "And for once we're not too interested in your p.m."

"Oh?" Standish straightened and his dark-blue eyes had humorous glints.

"Your job is to establish the cause of death, right? There can't be much doubt about that, can there, Doc?"

"I wouldn't say so. But you left out half the sentence."

"What sentence?"

"The one you quoted. 'To establish the cause of death . . .' You should have added: 'and determine if anyone is culpable.'"

"Culpable?" Cavanaugh snorted. "Hell yes, someone is culpable. Someone shot him in the heart, didn't they?"

"No gun?"

"No." Cavanaugh started to back toward the door and dismissed the subject. "We think the slug is just under the skin in his back. Must have clipped a bone."

"Did you move him?"

"We know better than that, Doctor," he said, emphasizing the last word. "We just bent him a little at the waist to see if the slug was in the chair. There's a small hard lump just under the skin. When you dig it out send it along, hunh?"

He went through the doorway without waiting for a reply and Standish took a large notebook from his bag. Opening it, he began to make a sketch. When Ballard asked him if it was all right to move the body, he said to give him a couple more minutes.

With the photographer out of the way, he penciled in a sketch of the room, noting the doors, windows, the chair, and the position of the body. He had no idea that this sketch, or the more detailed ones that would follow, would ever be used; it was simply part of a routine which had

been taught him by old Doc Lathrop, who had given him a
job as assistant in the days when he needed such fees, and
had groomed the younger man to take his place as medical
examiner before he retired. Ballard, a half smile on his face,
waited patiently because he had seen the routine before.
Not until Standish had turned toward the divan did he
speak to Sergeant Cooney, his assistant, and the detective
who had been standing by.

They began at once to empty the dead man's pockets,
placing the contents on a nearby table while the sergeant
listed each article in his own notebook. Standish, having
closed his bag, watched the photographer pack his para-
phernalia and spoke to Ballard.

"Any ideas?"

"Not many. Know him?"

"Jess Flemming."

"And the odds finally caught up with him."

"I know what you mean. I understand he was a bad boy."

"He'd been leaning on people for years, scaring little guys,
twisting their necks and sometimes breaking them."

"Did he have a record?"

"As long as your arm. But only three convictions. Two for
simple assault—he paid a fine—and one for felonious assault.
That time we had a case but he had a good mouthpiece.
Drew ninety days, suspended after thirty. That's all we
could ever tag him with around here."

Ballard grunted softly and continued in the same tone.
"Three times we had him up on suspicion of murder. The
first two times we didn't have a hell of a lot to go on and the
State's Attorney couldn't work up a case that would stick.
The third time we thought we had him. He worked over
this guy outside a bar. He shot him twice and we came up
with two witnesses. We knew he was guilty. We still know
it. The case is still on the books as an unsolved homicide."

He hesitated and Standish prodded him. "What happened?"

"We were giving this one witness pretty good protection and the other one we held as a material witness. The judge set bail at five thousand and it wasn't enough. Whoever was behind Flemming put it up and one fine day witness number one disappeared. Into thin air. He's still missing."

He cursed under his breath and said: "The five grand was a cheap price to pay, and with the pressure all on the other witness he suddenly got tongue-tied. Or maybe he got a sudden but permanent touch of amnesia. He had a convenient failure of memory. He wasn't sure any more. When the time came we couldn't even get an indictment."

"Who was Flemming doing all this strong-arm stuff for?"

"The loan sharks originally. The six-for-five boys. You know how that worked, don't you?"

Standish thought he did but he wanted to be sure. "You mean where some workingman needs five dollars on Monday to get through the week and when next Monday comes around he pays back six."

"Right. Or if he borrows fifty he pays back sixty. When he doesn't pay—in the beginning they don't care—the interest keeps adding up. Before long the poor guy is paying more in interest a week than the original loan.

"And it wasn't just the little guy you're talking about. There were small-businessmen who got themselves in a temporary bind. They'd need, say, five hundred or a thousand for a week or so. Sometimes they couldn't get it up when they thought they could. Before they knew it they'd be sweating just to keep up the interest. Maybe if it was a good little business the organization would wind up owning it."

"What organization?"

The question stopped Ballard and he gave it some thought, a moderately tall man about the same height as Standish but more solidly built and three or four years older. He had sandy hair and quick gray eyes that were often curious, prying, and observant. He dressed conservatively and in good taste and his suits were well tailored. He had a degree from a small upstate college and his face bore no visible marks of his trade. He was as tough as he had to be when the situation demanded and, if not brilliant, he was intelligent and well trained. He had one other quality that Standish had long admired, a basic integrity that could not be compromised. Now, his thinking completed, he answered as honestly as he could.

"I can't give you an exact answer. You read the papers. You've heard about the Mafia and the Cosa Nostra and the Syndicate. If you're wondering if such things exist, I think they do. On a nationwide basis, with territories—mostly in big cities—blocked off for the local big shots. Nowadays they have fronts that look respectable. They belong to clubs, and play golf, and own expensive boats. If you don't look too close, and don't know the background, you probably wouldn't recognize one if you fell over him. I understand they've taken over a lot of legitimate businesses, even banks.

"Well, this isn't New York or Boston. This is just a branch operation but there is a connection and there are three or four men here in town that call the shots in all the rackets, some of them petty, some of them not. We put the six-for-five boys out of business and the new state law they passed last year helped. That law's got teeth in it, so now they have a legitimate small-loan business with a charter. It's still profitable and muscle isn't used much any more. But we've got some unsolved murders on the books, obvious mob jobs. Boston has a raft of them. You got any idea how many?"

"No."

"Twenty-two."

"Twenty-two? In how long?"

"In the last seventeen months. The reason I know is that we just got a report on the last one. What the papers call another gangland slaying. Twenty-two," he said, sounding a little impressed himself. "They grab some guy as an accessory and he gets out on bail and two days later they find him in the back of a car or in some swamp. Most of them are small-timers but they know something, or somebody thinks they do. It's got to be gang stuff—somebody trying to cut in on somebody else—and the only reason I mention it is to give you the facts of life."

"So what about Flemming?"

"I wish I knew. He was out of town for a while. He came back with a new car. Somebody walked in here with a gun—" He fixed his gaze on Standish. "He could have been shot standing up and collapsed in the chair. He could have been sitting there when he got it. You couldn't tell, could you?"

"No. I can tell you the course of the bullet later but that probably won't help." Standish thought again of Ralph Estey and detoured mentally. "Flemming was in another jam four months ago."

"Yeah? What was that?"

"He ran over a man one Saturday night out in front of Hennessey's. My testimony kept him from facing a charge of vehicular homicide. Flemming was sober. The other man was staggering drunk."

"Umm." Ballard gave an unconscious nod of his head. "Sure. I remember now. The guy's name was Tremaine, wasn't it? A broker or a partner in some brokerage office as I recall it. His wife was with him and he came weaving out between two cars just as Flemming was starting up. Hit him and missed the wife, wasn't that it?" He eyed Standish aslant. "You got a point, Doc, or were you just thinking out loud?"

"Just thinking," Standish said, and then, bringing his thoughts back for the moment, he noticed that the sergeant and the detective had finished their tabulation and were standing by. He nodded toward the body in the chair. "Have you finished with him?"

Ballard said: "Yes. He's all yours. I don't think there's any hurry on the p.m. Any time tomorrow will do."

Standish stepped into the hall to summon the ambulance men and then he went along a small inner hall looking for a place to wash his hands. The kitchen was on the immediate right and he turned in here when he found the light on.

It was an oblong room, not large, and with one window. The refrigerator was an older model, its white enamel chipped. The electric stove was even older and not very clean. There were a few dishes and a cup on the drainboard and there was a rack for paper towels over the sink. A corroded soap dish was fastened above the faucets, and although he noticed that the smallish cake of soap was slightly damp when he picked it up, he did not think about it at the time.

He soaped his hands slightly with the water running, rinsed them, and reached for the roll of paper towels. He pulled two segments down and yanked them free. He blotted his hands and wadded the damp towel, glancing about for some place to discard it until he saw the wastebasket under the counter. Either he was careless or his aim was bad, for the ball of paper hit the rim of the basket and bounced to the floor.

A lifetime habit of personal neatness demanded that he retrieve the towel and put it where it belonged. It was this same characteristic neatness that took him one step more. For, having picked up the towel, he noticed a smaller folded piece of paper—apparently thrown there by someone else not quite so neat.

He reached for it instinctively, aware that if he had not hunkered down to get the towel he would not have seen the other paper at all because it was almost behind the metal basket and apparently had gone unnoticed by the person who had discarded it. Only when he had it in his hands and examined its whiteness and odd folds did he check his movement and take a second look. In this he was prompted, not by suspicion, but by a vague curiosity that had as its basis no more than a familiarity with other folded bits of paper of similar size, shape, and smoothness.

Curious now, still not suspicious, he opened the fold carefully. Holding the paper flat, he studied it a second or two and some trick of reflected light touched the residue of some powdery substance that had caught along the line of one fold. As he wondered about it he came erect, still holding the paper flat in one palm. He moved under the overhead light to get a better look.

He saw then that there were several grains of some colorless, crystalline substance and, automatically now, he brought the paper up under his nose and sniffed. He caught a faint odor which was not characteristic but aromatic. After another moment of silent contemplation, he isolated a grain. He touched it with the tip of his finger. When it stuck there he put it to his tongue. The slightly bitter taste that resulted was faint but unmistakable.

Very slowly then, he moved back to the counter and placed the paper down, a slender, erect-standing man of thirty-one, with dark hair and dark-blue eyes that were well spaced and direct. Because of a slight wave in his dark hair that could not be erased, he wore it rather short. His jaw was well cut and his angular face was longer than some, not handsome by classic standards, but with a smile that often came slowly and held a natural friendliness and sincerity easy to believe. For all his slenderness, there was a look of muscular fitness about him that was wiry and well coordinated, the shoulders good, the hips narrow.

For perhaps five seconds he stood immobile, his gaze somber and sightless as it fixed on some point above the sink. During that time he had no ears for the buzz of conversation or the restless movement in the adjoining room. When, finally, he brought his eyes to focus on the white paper in front of him, his thoughts moved on to consider Lieutenant Ballard. A moment later he knew it was time to call his friend's attention to his discovery.

4

WHEN PAUL STANDISH returned to the living room, Sergeant Cooney and the detective who had been there earlier were gone. Ballard was talking to another detective, a youngish, well-set-up man with prominent black brows and a muscular jaw. Standish had met him before and remembered that his name was Flint. Ballard, glancing round as Standish approached, nodded toward the detective.

"You know Johnny Flint, don't you? Well, it just might be that he's come up with something."

Standish waited, sensing from Ballard's calm but deliberate manner that Flint's information, whatever it was, was important and that it might be well to postpone any discussion of his recent discovery.

"Johnny stopped in Hennessey's Saturday night for a drink on his way home," Ballard said. "The doorman is a fellow who has been helpful from time to time in the past, and he just happened to mention that Flemming had some trouble there the night before."

"At Hennessey's?" Standish said, his mind leaping ahead and bracing itself for the disclosure he was afraid would follow.

"Yeah. Friday night. According to the doorman Flemming traded punches with the guy that plays the trumpet in the band."

"Ralph Estey?"

"That's the one."

"So?"

"So Johnny asked some questions, sort of passing the time of day but always interested in what Flemming might be doing, on account of his record and reputation. He also talked a little to Larry, the head barkeep. . . . You want to tell it?"

"I guess you know there's a real good-looking doll running the checkroom there," Flint said. "Sheila something or other."

"Keith," Standish said.

"Yeah. Blond, well-put-together. Greenish eyes that give you the big smile and a lot of false promises. Well, Estey's kind of sweet on her and Flemming had been horning in, trying to date the girl and being a nuisance, and Estey found out about it. They had some words and Estey made the mistake of trying to take on Flemming man to man. They went out on the sidewalk and it was a two-punch contest. Estey swung and Flemming, who must have outweighed the guy fifty pounds, flattened him. Estey hit his head on the sidewalk or curb. He was out cold. A doctor happened to be there and insisted on checking him over."

Flint stopped to glance at Ballard, who had been watching Standish. Standish was well aware of his steady gaze and was ready when the lieutenant finished the story.

"According to the doorman the doctor was you. You went across the street for your doctor's bag and then went inside to look Estey over."

"The doorman had it right," Standish said. "Estey had a concussion and I thought I'd better check."

"Umm." Ballard nodded slightly, his eyes thoughtful and full of doubt. "I'm a little surprised you didn't mention it."

There was an undertone of mild censure in the words and Standish could not quarrel with the statement. There was, he knew, some thought of Estey and the coincidental element of Friday night in the back of his mind, but he had kept it there. He was not sure whether this was deliberate or not and there was some evasion in his reply.

"I've been pretty busy, Tom," he said. "I remembered the fight but Captain Cavanaugh—and you seemed to go along —was pretty convinced that this was a simple gang killing or a deliberate attempt by someone who decided to pay Flemming off."

"That's exactly what I thought. If it wasn't for this Estey business I'd still think so."

"A man with Flemming's background and character must have made plenty of enemies."

"You know he did. He may have been doing some odd jobs for some of the big shots in town—we don't know about that yet—and if he double-crossed someone or tried to muscle in on somebody else's racket some hood could have walked in here on a contract and put him away. I've already got half a dozen men working on it. We're going to check Flemming out up, down, and sideways—where he's been, what he's been doing, who he's been seeing."

He paused again, rocking slightly on heel and toe. To Standish the pause seemed deliberate and the steady gray gaze narrowed slightly.

"There was one other little thing that Johnny forgot," Ballard added. "The doorman said something about Estey's making a threat. Johnny didn't pay much attention to it at the time but the way he heard it Estey said he had a gun and he was going to use it if Flemming gave him any more trouble. Did you hear anything like that?"

Standish had no further thoughts of evasion. In his own mind he could not picture the man he knew as Ralph Estey walking in here and cold-bloodedly shooting Flemming without further provocation. He was also well aware of his job and the ethical considerations involved.

"Yes," he said, "I did hear a threat. It didn't mean anything at the time because it was the kind of a thing any

man might say under the circumstances. I still think it was
nothing but talk, but I did hear it."

"Well, Johnny's going back and find his friend, the doorman. This time we'll get a proper statement but right now
I think I ought to have a word with that trumpet player
just in case. Do you know where he lives?"

Standish nodded, remembering his one visit to Estey's
room in a second-class hotel not far from the railroad station where the rates were modest and the clientele undis-
tinguished and not too prosperous.

"He has a room—or did have a couple of months ago—at
the Empire Hotel."

Ballard said "Good enough" and started to turn away but
Standish touched his arm and gestured toward the inner
hall.

"I found something in the kitchen that could be interesting. I think you ought to take a look before you leave."

He led the way after Ballard had sent Flint on his next
assignment. He pointed to the white piece of paper on the
counter. When Ballard started to reach for it, he stopped
him.

Ballard scowled first at the paper and then at Standish.
"Where did that come from? It wasn't there before."

"No."

"So what is it?"

"It's what they used to call a 'powder paper.'"

"Meaning?"

"Druggists use them to put up certain types of prescrip-
tions."

Ballard listened to the explanation, understanding it well
enough but not quite believing it.

"What the hell, Doc," he said. "I thought everything was
pills these days."

"Everything is—mostly," Standish said. "But Bromo
doesn't come in pill form, does it? Or Enos or Sal Hepatica.

You want something to dissolve quick in water, or any liquid for that matter, you don't use a pill, do you? You don't even use a capsule, which is the way most powder is contained these days. Even that takes time for the gelatin to dissolve."

He went on quickly then, explaining how he had washed his hands and thrown the towel at the wastebasket, how he had happened to spot the paper which had fallen near the baseboard.

"There are still a few grains stuck in one of the creases. Enough to analyze, I think."

Ballard's eyes were half closed now as he considered the paper and the problem it presented.

"You got any idea what it is? The powder, I mean?"

"I've got an idea. If you fold that paper carefully you can preserve the substance and take it over to Clem Jones, the city chemist. I'm pretty sure he can give you a definitive answer."

For a silent second or two Ballard seemed to be grappling with the idea. His expression suggested that he did not particularly care for the thought but he was a thorough and competent police officer and he understood that he could not ignore the possibility that Standish had presented.

"You say you know what it is? Okay, what?"

"It will only be a guess at this point," Standish said. "It isn't anything you could use in court."

"We're not in court, Doc. Come on," he added with some impatience, "there aren't any witnesses; I'm not going to quote you."

"My guess says that that paper contained chloral hydrate."

Ballard stared at him. "You mean the stuff they used to call 'knock-out drops'?"

"I guess you could say that," Standish said. "It may not be exact but it'll do."

THE RING OF TRUTH   35

"But even if you're right," Ballard persisted, unwilling as
yet to give credence to the doctor's theory, "the stuff could
have been used any time today or maybe even before. I
mean, Flemming may have had some broad up here and
slipped her a little something to make her more agreeable."

"Could be."

"I mean, it's possible, isn't it?"

"Sure it's possible," Standish said. "That's why I think I'd
better get hold of Dr. Emerson over at City Hospital and
do the autopsy tonight."

The idea seemed to startle Ballard. "Why tonight?
What's wrong with tomorrow morning? The guy was shot in
the heart, wasn't he?"

"Chloral hydrate is eliminated from the body very rapidly," Standish said. "If—and you notice I say *if*—Flemming
happened to take that chloral hydrate for any reason early
in the day I doubt if the autopsy would show any traces of
it. If, on the other hand, it was ingested shortly before he
was shot, Dr. Tracey, the pathologist, should be able to determine—"

"I know, I know," Ballard said. "You take out the stomach
and put it in a jar and seal it—"

"Along with the gastro-intestinal tract."

"—and Tracey takes a section of this and a section of that,"
Ballard continued as though there had been no interruption, "and eventually gives us the word. How long is that
going to take?"

"A while. It depends on how busy he is and when he can
get at it. Probably not before late tomorrow."

"I don't get it." Ballard shook his head. "It's like Cavanaugh said. Your job is to establish the cause of death and
determine if anyone is culpable and it looks like we already
got answers on both counts. Flemming was shot and somebody did it. So what's this—"

Standish knew what the lieutenant was going to say and

he cut him off. "It's just that I like to know the truth, Tom.
I think you do too. If there should happen to be chloral
hydrate in Flemming's system I think we ought to know
about it. I think we ought to find out why if we can."

Ballard started to say something and then stopped. For
he was thinking now as his mind went back over the years
he had known Standish, first as a resident at the hospital
and later as Dr. Lathrop's assistant. They'd had lunch together occasionally and now and then a friendly drink. He
had heard about the doctor's experience as an intern in New
York when he was riding ambulances and exchanging expe-
riences with various police officers who crossed his path.

He had heard more than once the two reasons Standish
had given for his interest in the medical examiner's job. As
a resident with nothing in the bank, the fees he earned
from assisting Lathrop had been important. He had also
quoted Lathrop's thoughts about the importance of a dis-
secting room in expanding a doctor's knowledge. "Good
surgeons," Lathrop had said, "cut swiftly, with long, sure
strokes, because they see in their minds the true picture of
the structure underneath. A good diagnostician should know
as much."

These were the two reasons Standish had quoted, but
Ballard was convinced there was a third, unspoken reason
—a basic interest in crime—that Standish had never admitted. A reason he had never put into words and, perhaps,
did not really understand himself. As chief medical examiner, a job he would relinquish in another year or so, he
was conscientious and dedicated. He had attended seminars
on forensic medicine at Harvard every year. He corre-
sponded with other medical examiners who were older and
more experienced, and he had clippings from journals which
stated the belief that homicides were involved in hundreds
of deaths each year that were passed off as natural because
of the lack of a proper medical-examiner law. He had

nothing against coroners, as such, whose job, too often of a patronage nature, was basically legal; but he felt that no unattended or suspicious death should be accepted as natural without a proper medical examination or post-mortem.

In the past Standish had helped Ballard on more than one occasion. He did not interfere with police work and it was usually Ballard who came to Standish when he needed help. At such times the only objection came from Mary Hayward, who resented the demands such work made on Standish's time. She had no inhibitions about telling Ballard what she thought and she insisted in a polite but continuing argument with Standish himself that he would be much better off in every way if he devoted all of his time to his own private practice. Let someone else do the medical examiner's job, was Mary's creed, and she was steadfast in her belief.

Ballard had never suggested that the doctor's persistence in learning the truth was due to this unspoken interest in crime. Since this was easy to deny, it was impossible to substantiate. He did not say so now. He merely took a deep breath and let it out through his lips.

"Okay, Doc," he said. "You want to stay up all night, that's your business. Just give me the cause of death in the morning and bring the slug with you."

He folded the "powder paper" very carefully and tucked it between two clean sheets of his pocket notebook.

"Me," he said, turning toward the door, "I want Ralph Estey. And maybe I should have a little chat with that hat-check girl. If it hadn't been for her there wouldn't have been any fight. Maybe she knows something that will help. What did you say her name was?"

"Sheila Keith."

"Would you know where she lives?"

Standish said no and followed the lieutenant from the room.

5

IT WAS after two before Paul Standish, with Dr. Emerson's assistance, had completed his part of the autopsy and made his notes. He was at his office at eight the next morning, and he had five house calls to make before he had time to stop at police headquarters. Now, going through the detectives' room on the second floor on his way to Lieutenant Ballard's small office, he saw Sheila Keith sitting at one end of a desk while a plainclothesman he did not know worked at a typewriter.

She was sitting erect in her chair, hands clenched in her lap. She was wearing a plaid woolen skirt and a beige sweater set, her plain navy coat over the back of the chair. She had a scarf over the ash-blond hair and her high-cheekboned face was pale and tense, her mouth compressed and marked with fatigue. The green eyes were dull and a little sick and she did not turn her head or notice him as he passed by. He saw all this as a doctor and wondered how much more pressure she could take before some sort of hysteria took over.

Lieutenant Ballard was slumped in his desk chair, his appearance suggesting that he had had even less sleep than Standish. His sandy hair was rumpled, so were his clothes. The shave he had given himself earlier must have been hurried and careless because traces of beard showed through. For all of this his greeting was friendly.

"Hi, Doc," he said. "Sit down."

Standish sat down and spoke directly. "How long have you had the Keith girl here? Not all night I hope?"

"No, why?"

"I was just wondering. She didn't even see me when I came in but I took a good look at her. I'd say she's had pretty nearly as much as she can take."

"Yeah?" Ballard considered the statement and tipped one hand. "Well, it's not our fault. We paid her a little visit last night around midnight and had to get her out of bed. She was pretty upset when she found out what happened and that we were looking for Estey."

"What did she say?"

"A lot of things, none of them very helpful. We asked her if she had seen Estey any time yesterday and she said no. We asked her if she'd been out during the evening and she said no. Hennessey's is closed on Mondays and she said she stayed home and washed out some things—there were some bras and stockings and panties hanging in the bathroom— and washed her hair. I told her we could talk some more this morning. I sent a car for her about nine o'clock."

"What did she tell you about Flemming?"

"Not much we didn't already know. She said she knew him in Florida last year. She said he was a persistent, annoying, and objectionable bully. She admitted there'd been a fight over her Friday night between Flemming and Estey but she said Estey wasn't the kind that would shoot anyone no matter what he said. And incidentally—"

Ballard leaned forward and slid his forearms across the desk. "We got a detailed statement from the doorman at Hennessey's and what Johnny Flint told us last night was about right. There was a little more but the substance of the story is the same."

"And what does Ralph Estey say about all this?"

"We don't know—yet."

"Oh?"

Ballard muttered something under his breath that sounded exasperated and profane.

"We haven't been able to pick him up. But we will. We've got the railroad station, bus terminal, and airport covered.

We've got stake-outs on Estey's room at the hotel, the girl's apartment; we're keeping an eye on Hennessey's in case he shows up there. We've even got a man on the ex-wife—her name is Johnson now."

Standish leaned back, his angular face grave and the dark-blue eyes full of thought. He had already telephoned the city chemist but he wanted to get the word from Ballard.

"What did Clem Jones have to say?"

"He said you were right. That 'powder paper' you found did contain traces of chloral hydrate. . . . You did the p.m.," he added defensively. "What did Flemming die from?"

"A gunshot wound."

"Sure. So there you are."

Standish reached into the change pocket of his jacket and brought forth the bullet he had removed from Flemming's back. He put it in the center of the blotter pad and watched Ballard pick it up and turn it between thumb and forefinger.

"A .32, hunh?" he said, and the words reminded Standish that Estey had said he owned a gun of that caliber on Friday night.

"You've been getting a rundown on Flemming," he said when Ballard finished his inspection. "Have you got any leads as to who might have walked in there and shot him like that? Have you found any gang connection?"

"No."

"Are you still checking?"

"Certainly, not that I expect it to do any good. Just give me Ralph Estey and I'll wrap it up for you. He had the motive—one of the best in the world—and if he's not involved, where is he?"

"Did you go over Flemming's apartment?"

"All the way."

"Did you find any gun?"

"No."

"What about the chloral hydrate."

"You keep saying that," Ballard said, his exasperation showing, "and all I can say is, what about it?"

"Suppose Dr. Tracey comes up with a finding that Flemming *did* ingest chloral hydrate shortly before his death. Can you figure a good reason why Estey would have wanted to use it? It would have to be given in food or drink, probably a drink."

"It could be figured."

"Okay. Go ahead. Give it a try. Let's take a hypothetical situation. Estey calls on Flemming with a gun in one pocket and the chloral hydrate in the other. I'll be Flemming and you be Estey. Give me some dialogue."

"Okay," Ballard said. "But you be Flemming and I'll be Estey. You're sitting around your apartment and you hear a knock on the door. You open it up and you see me—Estey —standing there. Go ahead, talk."

"What do you want you dirty little sneak?"

"I just want to talk to you, Jess. That business Friday night was pretty silly. You and I are intelligent men, and we ought to be able to work something out. Okay to come in?"

"So I let you in," Standish said. "Then what?"

"Then I say 'How about a drink? Let's relax and sit down and talk this over in a friendly way. I'll help you; where's the whiskey, in the kitchen?'"

Standish grunted; then grinned at the lieutenant's persistence. "So we go out into the kitchen and you dump the chloral hydrate into my glass when I'm not looking. This presupposes that Estey, intent on murder, is afraid to walk in on Flemming and do the job."

"It could have happened that way," Ballard said stubbornly. "Estey was a little guy and he was afraid of Flemming. For all he knew Flemming might be carrying a gun too. If he took a quick shot and missed a vital part Flemming would take care of him. If he can put Flemming to sleep he's got no problem. One shot, dead center, and the job is done."

Ballard gave emphasis to his words but they lacked conviction and he seemed to realize it. He leaned back, his grin crooked.

"It could happen that way," he repeated.

"But you don't really believe it."

"If anybody fed Flemming chloral hydrate in a drink it was probably that dame outside."

Standish matched Ballard's grin with one of his own. "She cons Flemming into taking the drink and then Estey walks in later, fires the shot, and walks out again. That's real good too."

"It's better than the other." Ballard sat up again. "But right now I say to hell with it. Just give me Estey and write out your report, with or without chloral hydrate. Let the State's Attorney and the County Detective take it from there."

"I have one other thought," Standish said, "and I might as well get it off my chest. You can say it's farfetched, tenuous, and wild, but bear with me a couple of minutes longer. You've heard me sound off about the necessity for a universal medical-examiner law with a qualified doctor on call whenever an autopsy is suggested or needed."

"I have," Ballard said dryly. "According to you—and I'm not saying you're wrong, understand—thousands of people are buried each year with a death certificate saying they died of heart failure or a stroke or some other thing when in reality they've been poisoned."

"Exactly. Not by cyanide or anything that could be easily detected, but over a period of time and systematically. Such cases crop up in the newspapers from time to time but there are hundreds of others that never make it. There's also one other simple method of murder that the public knows less about."

"If you mean hit-and-run cases, you're right. The racketeers have used that method for years."

"Because the state laws are set up for it," Standish said. "It doesn't have to be hit-and-run either. Let's just call it vehicular homicide. Say you're married. You hate your wife and you're in love with another woman, with no chance of a divorce. You might even inherit some money. But if you hit her with a car and kill her the motive is easily established, and you're up on murder one or two and you get put away for twenty years to life. For that reason, in the cases I'm talking about, a third party is generally involved."

"Sure," Ballard said. "You hire someone. That's the way the mobsters did it."

"Someone who never saw your wife until you point her out. And there's basically two ways of handling it. You pick an average sort of a guy to do the job but you make sure that if he has a record it's a petty one. He runs down your wife on a busy street. He stops the car and gives what aid he can. He's arrested on one charge or another, but when the case comes up, since there's no connection whatsoever between this man and your wife, it has to go down as an accident. The worst the guy will get will be reckless driving or some such citation, which means all they'll hand him is a fine and possibly loss of his license.

"The other way," he added, "the one you're talking about, is where a hoodlum steals a car, does a hit-and-run job, and keeps going for half a mile or so until he can abandon the car. There isn't one chance in ten that the police will ever nail him, and even if his luck is bad, even if he crashes the car and gets caught, what does he say in court? I'll tell you.

"He says that maybe he was drunk or that he panicked after the accident. But even if they could prove driving while drunk they couldn't put him away for more than a year or two. . . . Because that's the law," Standish said, persisting. "Because every guy on the jury understands that the same thing might happen to him someday. Even with proven negligence—"

"Sure. Sure." Ballard's impatience was beginning to show and he pushed his chair back and stood up. "So what's bugging you, Doc? What's the point? I've heard this before, not the same line but the same general theme."

"I told you the idea was farfetched," Standish said. "But I was at Hennessey's Friday night, as you know. After the fight I was sitting at the bar and I remembered the Saturday night four months ago when Jess Flemming ran over a man out front named Robert Tremaine. For just a second I wondered if it was a matter of simple coincidence."

"What do you mean, coincidence?"

"Flemming was at Hennessey's. So were the three people closest to Tremaine."

"What three people?"

"Tremaine's widow—I think her name is Evelyn—and his former partner, Warren Choate, had been there for dinner. Tremaine's brother, Donald, apparently joined them for a drink but he came down the street outside just in time to see that fight."

"So it was a coincidence," Ballard said. "What about it? Just what the hell are you driving at?"

Standish stood up and allowed himself a small grin.

"I'm not sure. Maybe it's just the suspicious mind I have. Or maybe too much imagination. I've been thinking that it *might* be possible that someone could have hired Flemming to stage that accident. Do you want the facts as I remember them?"

Ballard had been looking out the lone window with his back to the room and now he turned and shook his head.

"No," he said succinctly but with no irritation. "All I want right now is Ralph Estey. Let me have my little session with him first. If I can't hang this on him, if there's any doubt in my mind, that will be time enough to listen to the rest of your—did you say farfetched?—theory and your facts. Okay?"

Standish said: "All right." He moved over to the door, then turned, his hand still on the knob.

"What about the Keith girl?"

"What about her?"

"I told you I thought she had about as much as she could take."

"What have you got in mind?"

"Well—if you don't have to hold her I thought I might take her home and give her a couple of pills. She'll make more sense if she has a chance to relax."

Ballard listened with respect. "Sure," he said. "I don't want any trouble with her. She ought to be finished by now. Let's see."

Sheila Keith was still in the chair at the end of the desk. She seemed not to have moved a muscle since Standish had last seen her. Her face was pale and drawn, but when he stopped beside her and she glanced up, the green eyes opened and a tired smile began to work on them and the lines of her mouth.

Ballard asked the detective if she had finished and the man said: "Just about, Lieutenant. I was sort of waiting for you."

"That will be all for now, Miss Keith," Ballard said. "And thanks for your cooperation. Dr. Standish has offered to drive you home if that's all right with you."

The girl made no immediate answer but got to her feet and Standish held her coat for her.

"Keep thinking about Ralph Estey, Miss Keith," Ballard said in parting. "If he should happen to get in touch with you you'll be doing him a favor if you let us know. . . . See you, Doc. Keep after Tracey. If he comes up with anything give me the word, okay?"

c

6

SHEILA KEITH walked from the room with Standish at her side, and he kept his hand lightly on her arm as they went down the steps and out back of the headquarters building where his car was parked. When she settled herself in her seat her firm, determined chin was up and she seemed to be making a deliberate effort to keep her emotions under control. She made no comment and gave no outward sign that she was aware of him until he maneuvered the car out on the street.

"It's my fault," she said finally.

Standish, his attention on the traffic pattern, made no reply. He knew there was more to come and waited until she continued.

"I don't mean about Flemming. What happened to him doesn't surprise me much. If anyone ever had it coming to him, he did."

"According to Ballard he had a record of violence going back quite a while."

"I don't know much about what he did here but I know what he was like in Florida. I've been around enough to know how to handle bullies like him. At least that's what I thought. Maybe I should have gone to the police when he started to bother me. If I hadn't been so stupid, if I hadn't mentioned it to Ralph, he wouldn't have got involved; there wouldn't have been any fight; the police wouldn't be looking for him. And they're wrong. I told them so. Ralph didn't kill Jess Flemming. He wouldn't kill anybody."

"Then where is he?"

"How do I know?" she said, her voice a little shrill. "He's

a musician. Who knows what they do when they're not working?"

"You heard him make that threat Friday night. So did the doorman. He happened to tell a detective named Flint about it and—"

"It didn't mean a thing." She drew her coat more tightly across her breasts. "Everybody makes threats if they get mad enough. I've made them myself. Haven't you?"

Standish was not sure how to answer this and as he hesitated she went on in the same flat, matter-of-fact tone.

"Ralph was hurt and humiliated."

"He'd had a good crack on the back of the head too."

"He was still a little stunned; he must've been. He probably didn't know what he was saying."

"I talked with him later," Standish said. "He said he had a gun. Did you know that?"

"I heard what he said on the sidewalk about carrying one. I thought it probably was just talk."

Standish pulled up at a traffic light and glanced at the girl, seeing her face in profile and noting again the tension that shaped it.

"We talked some about you," he said. "Did you know Ralph was in love with you?"

"That depends upon what you mean by *know*."

"Didn't he ever say so?"

"Not in so many words, but with musicians that doesn't mean much. About all they talk about is their work, and the dates they've got lined up, the money they're going to make, and what they're going to do next year."

"You told me you thought he was wonderful."

"And I meant it. Ralph did a lot for me. He went to bat with Mr. Hennessey for me. He made a couple of good arrangements—for free—when I thought I was going to continue singing. He put in a word for me on the checkroom job. He was kind and considerate and polite. He never pushed or tried to wrestle me into the bed after he'd had a couple of drinks. But we never really talked seriously. About us, I mean. He never asked me to marry him—"

"And if he had?"

"Well—" She let the word dangle and leaned back in her corner of the seat, her chin tucked in the collar of her coat now and some new distance in the green eyes. "I guess I would have told him no," she said quietly. "Not because I didn't like him, you understand. It's just that—well—marrying a musician, any musician, wasn't part of my plans. I don't mean that some of them are not real nice guys or that they don't do pretty good. But I was married to one once, so maybe I'm prejudiced."

"Oh?" Standish waited for perhaps three seconds and then prompted her. "How long ago was that?"

"Four years ago. I was nearly twenty-one and old enough to know better. Because I'd been on my own since I was eighteen and I'd been exposed to entertainers of all kinds enough to understand something about the breed.

"I was never real poor," she added, some far-off quality in her voice now. "Sort of middle-class, I'd guess you'd call it; maybe a little on the lower-middle-class side. My father ducked out when I was quite young but my mother was a hard worker—she worked up to be the dietitian of a small hospital in Ohio and she was ambitious for me. I took dancing lessons, including ballet, ever since I can remember. There were even a few on baton twirling so I could be a drum majorette. There were also piano lessons for a little while but they didn't take. She forced me—in the beginning, I mean—to try out for every high-school play that came along. Pretty soon I didn't need any urging. I did a little singing with a local band when I was a senior. When she died suddenly not long after graduation there wasn't much money and I had to make up my mind. I couldn't type, and I didn't know shorthand, and I didn't want to stand on my feet all day clerking behind some counter. So"—she gave a

small shrug to her shoulders—"I decided I might as well
keep on going the way my mother had headed me."

She took a deep breath and let it out. When she continued there was a sardonic inflection to her words.

"New York, naturally. The big town. I wasn't sure just
what line my career was going to take but I was on my way.
I made the rounds just like ten thousand other girls with
not much more than average ability. When the money ran
out I went to work because when I want something I don't
give up easily. I'm not built that way. I was an usherette,
and a waitress, and, during the summer, a carhop out on
Long Island. I took on all the free meals I could and what
I saved I spent on more dancing lessons. For a while, that is.
I even went to drama school for six months, thinking I might
make it as an actress. The best I could do was some walk-
ons and a lot of stagehand work for a summer-stock company.

"But when you move around the way I did you meet a
lot of people. They're all types and I've seen most of them.
Dancers—boys and girls—singers, agents, bookers, musicians
—especially musicians. Too many of them no-talent characters but they all have one thing in common: they're going
to make it big someday in some form of the entertainment
business. Now and then I picked up a few dollars singing
with small-time bands, mostly club dates out in the sticks.
When one of these groups got a booking in Florida I went
along."

She sighed again and pulled herself erect on the seat. For
the first time she looked at Standish, and when he glanced
at her and saw the small, wry smile he knew that her con-
fession had been a therapeutic which had erased some of
the tension from her mind and from her face.

"So I married a piano player," she said in the same sardonic tone. "This was in Florida. He was a tall good-looking
guy, very smooth, a born liar, and he gave me a first-class
snow job. I can't remember how I felt at the time; it was too

long ago. I can't believe that I could fall for the line he put out, but maybe I was just too tired of knocking myself out all alone. He had a five-piece combo and Friday and Saturday nights I did some singing. I moved my things into his apartment. A real big deal. The trouble was he wasn't home very often and when he was he'd get crocked and start slapping me around. But why bore you with the sorry details? I'd rather forget it."

Standish, turning into the street where his office was located, and wanting to hear the rest of it, said: "What happened?"

Her smile was a little more in evidence now but it was still crooked around the mouth.

"You mean to make a long story short? Actually, it's very simple. I finally wised up. I wanted a divorce and he said okay but he wouldn't give me a dime. So one weekend when he went off on a boat with a party of friends—a mixed group, I might add—I cleaned out the apartment. I invited a secondhand dealer in and I sold everything he'd take. My husband's clothes—what he hadn't taken with him—the television, his high-fi set, his recorder. I left him his precious records and took off. I hocked my engagement ring for a hundred bucks—a diamond with about ninety-six flaws in it. I holed up in a town in Alabama long enough to get my divorce and I haven't seen my ex-husband since." She laughed abruptly as she finished. "Maybe I'm not doing so great as a single," she said. "But at least this way I'm my own woman."

The frank and uninhibited disclosure of her past told Standish a lot about this girl and what made her tick, but he was still not satisfied.

"How much of this does Ralph know?"

"Quite a bit. I never made a production number out of it like I just did with you, but I guess it came out here and there in bits and pieces. Just like he'd tell me about himself from time to time, and how it was with him and his wife. . . . I had nothing to do with that divorce, you know," she added quickly. "That was all in the books before I came here. From what Ralph said they'd been separated quite a while."

She hesitated and said: "Maybe she looked at that marriage the same way I would if he actually asked me. She'd given it a try. She at least had a child. She must have figured out there was no future in it any longer. Why should there be for me? I don't mean that Ralph couldn't still make it. He's good. He always has been. He had a lot of drive."

"He still has."

"He doesn't have Bobby Hackett's tone," she said as though she had not heard, "but who has? Maybe Ruby Braff's lower-register work is a little better but Ralph is an all-around trumpet man. Anyone who ever worked with him can tell you that. He can do anything. Also he's a pretty fair country arranger. No Neal Hefti maybe, but sound. You know? But—where does he go from here?

"Maybe," she added, very earnest now, "Ralph wasn't tough enough. I mean, in any part of the entertainment business, you have to *learn* to be tough. You do what you have to do, and never mind who gets hurt. If you don't everybody will push you around and you'll wind up wondering what happened to all your dreams."

Standish knew what she meant and thought she had expressed herself very well. He also remembered something that Estey had told him Friday night. "He told me the other night that he had some things lined up."

"Good horn players like Ralph always have things lined up, according to them. He said he had a couple of record dates on tap for this summer and I know he's been talking with a couple of jazz buffs in Boston. Rich kids—you know, amateurs—who are thinking about opening a spot up there. I don't know whether it's supposed to be a new place or whether they hope to buy out another club. The idea is to put in someone to handle the food and let Ralph take over the band and the entertainment. . . . I don't mean to say

I'd never marry Ralph," she said. "But right now—I mean, the way things are—I wouldn't, no. I don't think he expects me to. . . . What are we stopping here for?"

Standish had pulled up in front of the remodeled brick house that served as offices for him and four other doctors.

"This is where my office is," he said, and grinned at her. "Across the hall you'll find a pediatrician and a urologist. Upstairs two psychiatrists."

"But—I thought you were going to take me home."

"I am. But first I want to give you a couple of capsules that will relax you a little. . . . Come on," he said, walking round the car and opening the door on her side. "I'd like you to meet my girl Friday, Mary Hayward. It won't take but a minute or two and after that we'll take you home. Okay?"

Mary Hayward was sitting behind her desk in a corner of the reception room which was set apart on one side by a glass partition. She stood up when she spotted Standish and said, formally: "Good morning, Doctor." At the same time and before Standish could make any introduction, she took a quick but all-inclusive look at Sheila Keith that seemed to assess her from head to toe.

"Mary, this is Sheila Keith—Mary Hayward. . . . You remember Sheila from Hennessey's, don't you?"

"Certainly," Mary said, and offered a guarded smile. "How are you?"

"Hello, Mary. I'm not quite sure I know how I am," Sheila said, returning the smile. "The doctor seems to think I need some sort of tranquilizer. At least that's what he said."

Standish had left the office before Mary Hayward came on duty but he had talked to her over the telephone and she knew about the autopsy he had performed as well as the essential facts of the murder of the night before.

"The police have been looking for Ralph Estey," Standish said. "You know, the trumpet player that leads the band at Hennessey's."

"Oh?" Mary's brow furrowed slightly as she looked again at Sheila. "Because they think he had something to do with the murder?"

"They don't know," Standish said. "They just want to question him. So far they haven't been able to locate him. . . . Estey's a friend of Sheila's, and Lieutenant Ballard's had her down at his office most of the morning."

"They insist on thinking that Ralph must have had something to do with it," Sheila said. "I keep telling them he didn't but they're awfully hard to convince."

She continued to add to her own denial while Standish excused himself and went into his examining room, where he opened a glass cabinet and found a bottle of capsules. He tipped two into his hand and replaced the bottle. He put one capsule into a small envelope and kept the other in his palm while he got a glass of water.

"Take this one now," he said when he went back to Sheila. "You can take the other before you go to work." He handed her the envelope. "Or maybe you don't feel like working tonight. Is there anyone who could take over for you?"

"Madge Kane could handle it, I guess. She's been helping me out Saturday nights the last couple of months, but— no, I don't think so." She shook her head to give emphasis to her decision. "I'd rather work. It's a lot better than sitting home and doing nothing."

"I told Sheila I'd run her home, Mary," Standish said. "I'll be right back."

Mary Hayward frowned and this time she was the one who shook her head. When on duty she was very jealous of the doctor's time, his prerogatives, and possibly his affections. The reminder she now gave him was pleasant but firm.

"You have appointments starting at one, Doctor." She glanced at her wristwatch. "It's twelve-thirty now. Have you had anything to eat?"

"Well"—the directness of this reminder flustered him momentarily and he hesitated—"no. I can order a sandwich sent over from the corner drugstore."

"Yes," Mary said. "You do that and I'll run Miss Keith home."

"Nobody has to run me home," Sheila said. "No, I mean it," she added to forestall any protest. "I only live two blocks from here." She looked at Standish and smiled. "As a matter of fact, my place is on the street in back of you. Don't you keep your car in that row of garages in the alley between the two streets?"

"Yes," Standish said, having no idea until now where the girl lived.

"So do I. I thought I'd seen you drive out of there." She buttoned her coat and tucked her handbag under her arm as she backed toward the door. "It's a nice day and I could use the exercise. I've done nothing but sit ever since that police car came to get me. . . . Good-by, Miss Hayward." She nodded and now she gave Standish the practiced smile he had noticed so often at Hennessey's. "And thank you, Doctor. I'm beginning to feel better already."

7

MARY HAYWARD stood for a moment watching the door Sheila Keith had closed. She was clad in nurse's white, since Standish could not yet afford a nurse and a secretary, but the uniform detracted not at all from her firmly rounded figure that was more slender than buxom but definitely not boyish. Her legs were trim and shapely and her complexion could stand on its own, with or without makeup. She had medium-brown hair, gray eyes, and a no-nonsense manner while on duty. But this could change when the occasion demanded, making her a softly feminine and altogether charming young lady who would be twenty-four on her next birthday.

Now, turning, the gray eyes speculative as she watched Standish, she said: "She's very attractive, isn't she?"

Standish sensed some challenge here but he was not sure why. "Well—yes. I think so."

"Smart too, I'll bet."

"She's been around, if that's what you mean."

"Then maybe 'experienced' is a better word. Did she talk much on her ride over?"

"Quite a lot." Standish grinned and decided it might be wise to change the subject. "What about my sandwich?"

"I'll order it right now," she said, and reached for the telephone. "What kind?"

"I don't know. I'm not too hungry. A tuna-fish on white, I guess. Milk. Have you eaten?"

"No." She smiled ingenuously. "I thought I'd wait for you —I mean, in case you decided to have something sent in."

She dialed a number, gave Standish's order, asked for a ham-on-rye and coffee for herself. This told Standish he was in for an inquisition of sorts, a confidential chat during which the normal doctor-nurse relationship was suspended as if by mutual consent. He smiled inwardly at the thought. He was glad that there would not be much time, and he was ready when she laid out the sandwiches and poured his milk.

For it was Mary's custom to take a specified hour for lunch, usually in the company of some friends who worked in the neighborhood. Normally she kept her curiosity in hand regarding his patients. She did not ask improper questions or attempt to discuss their problems, ailments, or treatment. This lack of curiosity did not always apply to Standish's duties as a medical examiner even though she was outspoken in her disapproval of such activities. At such times she contrived, for one reason or another, to decide on a sandwich in the office. The way she managed it was always quite fortuitous and there was never any suggestion that she was deliberately making the opportunity for confidential sessions.

This time she had heard about the murder and wanted to know more. The appearance of Sheila Keith had apparently whetted her appetite for information, and as Standish answered her opening questions he found himself mentally comparing the two girls.

From what Sheila had told him, she was about a year older than Mary. Each girl was most attractive in her own way, though Mary's prettiness, perhaps because of her background, was less artificial and more wholesome. It occurred to him that Sheila might be more exciting but since this was only conjecture on his part he did not dwell on it now.

Mary had come from New Hampshire. By the time she finished high school, her father, a widower, was a semi-invalid and Mary had worked in the town library so she could contribute to the family income and at the same time keep house for her father. A small-town lawyer, he had been a long-time friend of Dr. Lathrop's, and when he died it was Lathrop who suggested that Mary might try nursing as a career.

Taking his suggestion, she had come to Union City. She had had one year as a student nurse when an attack of hepatitis which was unusually persistent forced her to drop out. By the time she had fully recovered, Standish was about to open his office and again it was Lathrop who recommended Mary for the one-woman job, all that Standish could afford at the time.

Now, having learned the details of last night's murder and the altercation over Sheila Keith that had preceded it on Friday night, she gathered the wax paper from the sandwiches and stuffed it into the cardboard containers. When she had discarded them and made sure there were no crumbs about, she glanced at her watch.

"Mrs. Davis is first," she said. "She wanted to discuss her hypertension with you."

Standish nodded, but his recent recital of details involving the Flemming murder had revived his interest and his doubts and now, deciding he would take one more unofficial step, he said:

"When you get a chance, and the sooner the better, Mary, I want you to set up an appointment for me in my office at the morgue. Make it between four-thirty and five if you can. I'd like to see Mr. and Mrs. Warren Choate. You can try their residence for her and his office for him. Choate & Tremaine. Elm Street, I think. The City National Bank Building." He waited while she made the notation on her pad. "Also Mrs. Robert Tremaine. I think her first name is Evelyn. And Donald Tremaine. He's a C.P.A. with Roberts & Waterman. You'll find them in the book."

Mary had it all down before she looked at him and suddenly there was a glimmer of doubt and suspicion in the gray eyes.

"Oh," she said.

"Oh what?"

"I think I remember the names. Weren't some of those people involved in that accident outside Hennessey's last December?"

"They were. Mrs. Tremaine's husband was run down and killed."

"By a man named Flemming." Her eyes were suddenly startled and intent. "You're not saying this is the same Flemming that—"

"The same, Mary."

She was still watching him but she seemed to have trouble digesting this new discovery and finding a proper reply.

"But what—" She tried again. "I mean—do you think there's any connection between that accident and—"

"I don't know."

"But you must think something like that."

"Not think, Mary. I'm just wondering. I'd sort of like to see them again."

"You can't ask them officially, can you?"

"Probably not. But they don't know that."

"Suppose I can't locate all of them?"

"Then do the best you can."

"But what can I say to them?" she said, still resisting. "What excuse do I give?"

It was a good question and because Standish had no ready answer he had to feel his way along.

"Just say I'm reviewing the case before filing it. Or that I want corroboration on one or two points before closing the case. Something like that. Make it sound as if they're doing me a favor."

Mary straightened her shoulders and smoothed down her uniform but her own uncertainty still showed in her face.

"All right, Doctor," she said, formal once more. "But would you mind telling me why? That case is already closed. You said so yourself. It was your testimony at the hearing that made it possible."

Standish had not mentioned the chloral hydrate to Mary and he did not do so now.

"Maybe Flemming's death reopened it," he said evenly. "I don't think that murder is as cut and dried as Ballard would like to believe. There was considerable insurance money involved in Robert Tremaine's death. I remember something about it because the insurance adjusters questioned me. Let's just say I'd like to refresh my memory."

He glanced at his watch, making the gesture obvious and deliberate to stop any further questioning.

"Who did you say was first on the book? Mrs. Davis? You might see if she's here."

Mary knew when she was dismissed but she did not give up easily. She stopped at the door to consult her notebook.

"All right, Doctor," she said primly. "But you'll not forget the Jordan boy's throat, will you? I told his mother you'd stop in sometime later this afternoon."

"Okay, I'll see him."

"And Mrs. Lathrop."

"Mrs. Lathrop," he said with some exasperation.

"She's very wealthy," Mary Hayward said. "She has wealthy friends. She's complaining about some new pain around her heart."

"And shortness of breath. Because she stuffs herself and won't exercise or follow the diet I gave her."

"You'll go see her, though. I told her you would. And Mrs. Naylor called again this morning."

"No, Mary, I will not."

"But, Doctor."

Standish grinned crookedly. "There's nothing wrong with her stomach. What she needs is a psychiatrist and I told her so. Her trouble is nothing more than an ingrown streak of jealousy combined with a guilt complex that crops up when she misbehaves. If she calls again tell her you'll make an appointment for her with Dr. Mason upstairs. . . . Will you ask Mrs. Davis to step in, please?"

8

THE MORGUE in Union City was a small red-brick building with a granite-trimmed entrance. Two and a half stories high and built like a cube with no distinguishing features, it stood adjacent to the hospital complex. A ramp discreetly located at the back gave access to the basement, which was half aboveground, and stone steps with wrought-iron railings led to the main floor, where the city had provided offices for the medical examiner and his official files. To the left of the entrance hall was a seldom-used record room, and stairs led to the second floor, which was divided between the autopsy rooms and the city chemist's laboratory.

Paul Standish's principal domain was on the right, a modest two-room suite no different from thousands of other small business enterprises. The outer office, occupied at present by a middle-aged spinster secretary, had a solid wall of green-metal filing cabinets and now, at ten minutes to five, Standish, having seen both the Jordan boy and Mrs. Lathrop, stopped in front of her desk.

"Mrs. Tremaine, Donald Tremaine, and Mr. Choate are inside."

"Have they been here long?"

"Just a few minutes. . . . Oh, yes, and Mary phoned to say she had been unable to locate Mrs. Choate."

Standish discarded his hat and coat, and as he turned to the door of his private office, he recalled his earlier conversation with Mary Hayward and remembered her look of shock and surprise when he told her what he had in mind. Until now he'd been too busy to wonder what he was going to say or what he expected to prove, and for the first time a definite sense of doubt and uncertainty made itself felt.

At the moment, had there been a chance, he would have backed away from this meeting. One part of his brain told him to forget the whole thing but the other part, the medical-examiner part, kept telling him that it was his job to know the truth no matter where the search took him. There was perhaps another factor. This, although he probably did not recognize it, was a perverse desire to ignore the simple facts of murder as Ballard had them. There was a second or two when it occurred to him that this desire was ill-founded, but even as such thoughts undermined his determination, he realized he no longer had any alternative. And so, taking a small breath and putting on what he hoped would be a bland and businesslike expression, he opened the door.

He saw at once that Evelyn Tremaine and Warren Choate had appropriated the one leather divan that stood opposite the windows. Donald Tremaine had a matching chair diagonally across from them. They all looked up as he entered and he nodded politely and said good afternoon.

They said: "Good afternoon, Doctor," almost in unison as he went round the desk and sat down.

He had taken the Tremaine file from the other room early that morning after he had finished the post-mortem. He had glanced through it briefly before putting it in the center drawer of the desk. Now, as he spread the papers before him, he took a second, all-inclusive glance at the trio.

If he had not seen Evelyn Tremaine on two or three occasions previously, not counting her Friday-night appearance at Hennessey's, he probably would have let his glance linger on her face a little longer because she was, in every respect, worth a second look. He remembered her as being uncommonly attractive, and the word that came to him was "striking." For she was a statuesque, high-breasted woman, beautifully turned out now in her tailored black suit and white blouse.

Her skin was creamy and artfully made up. Her eyes looked black under the carefully arched brows and her hair had the shiny, almost iridescent blackness of a crow's back in sunshine. To make it more noticeable, she wore it simply, in a smooth, drawn-back fashion, with a small bun at the neck, giving her somehow a classic look that complemented the almost symmetrical planes and angles of her face; a coldly beautiful face somehow, yet one which to Standish seemed to promise a reserve of warmth and mobility if one could find the proper stimuli.

"I appreciate your coming, Mrs. Tremaine," he said, looking right at her this time. "I'm sorry I have to bring up what must be a tragic memory for you."

He shuffled the papers in the manila folder, still not sure how to proceed. Warren Choate's question did not help any.

"Is this some sort of post-mortem inquiry?"

"Well, in a sense, yes."

"And you're acting in your official capacity as medical examiner?"

"I guess you could say that."

Standish was still trying to play an unfamiliar melody by ear. He fooled with his typewritten sheets and when he thought he was overdoing the bit he leaned back and fixed his eyes on the molding of the ceiling.

"But as you can see, there's no stenographer present and I'm not asking for any formal statements. Your coming here is—I hope my secretary's remarks over the telephone when she called you were not construed as a summons—a favor and I hope you will indulge me in my curiosity."

This was quite a mouthful for a normally reticent man, but, having delivered it, he immediately felt better and was somehow more sure of himself. He considered Warren Choate briefly, a prosperous, sturdily built man in his early or middle forties, with thick graying hair and a forceful manner. His blocky face was ruggedly attractive and had a definite tan that came either from some recent southern trip or from the more constant application of a sun lamp.

"My secretary was not able to locate your wife."

"Neither was I," Choate said. "Your girl asked for her telephone number. She could be out of town for the day. As a matter of fact, I haven't seen her myself lately. We've been separated for two months. There's a divorce in the works if we can agree on a financial settlement. But what could she have to do with this discussion?"

"Probably nothing. It's just that she was with you the night of the accident. There were four of you at Hennessey's, as I remember. You and Mrs. Choate, and you"—he glanced again at Evelyn Tremaine—"and your husband. It was sort of a regular thing, wasn't it? I mean, the four of you going out for dinner Saturday nights."

"Most Saturdays, yes," Choate said. "Bob and I were partners and pretty good friends and we usually got together once a week or so."

Standish considered his report and then glanced at Donald Tremaine, who had slouched well down in his chair and had been listening politely but with no particular interest. About Choate's height but more delicately built, he wore metal-rimmed spectacles that magnified slightly his pale-blue eyes. His light-brown hair was worn a bit long and he had, somehow, a lean, ascetic look.

"According to your testimony, you weren't at Hennessey's at all that night," Standish said.

"That's right. There was a movie I wanted to see."

Outside, a tractor-trailer labored through its lower gears and a horn sounded a warning as tires squealed briefly with a sudden application of brakes. Here there was only the sound of the typewritten sheets as Standish stacked them together and evened the edges.

"My examination, if you may remember, showed that Mr. Tremaine was quite drunk."

"He was looped," Evelyn Tremaine said flatly.

"More so than usual, for a Saturday night?"

"I wouldn't say so." She crossed her knees and smoothed her skirt. "My husband was just one of those men who drank pretty consistently, but only on his Saturday nights out did he carry the habit to excess. He had business luncheons several days a week. Warren can tell you about that."

"He was a three-Martini man," Choate said, "but it never seemed to show much."

"Three more before dinner—when he was home," the woman added. "Maybe a brandy or two afterward. Sometimes a highball. I guess he was adjusted to that amount of alcohol because he always seemed alert and in good spirits

the next morning. Saturdays he had this habit." She tipped
one long-fingered hand. "He went out to enjoy himself and
to Robert that meant all the whiskey after dinner he could
handle and for as long as the law allowed."

Standish nodded and spoke to Choate. "You and your wife
left early that night, I believe."

"That's right. Marion, my wife, was getting a little fed up
with these Saturday-night excursions anyway. We'd been
doing this sort of thing for years and in the beginning I
guess it was all right with her. I was like Robert in a way.
I liked to unwind on Saturday nights and if there was a
dinner dance at the Country Club we'd go there or, during
the summer, maybe to the Yacht Club. Other times we'd go
to Hennessey's. Marion didn't drink much anyway and the
idea of sitting up half the night with people who did no
longer amused her. She went because I wanted to go and
that particular night Robert started kidding her about something and she didn't like it."

"He was like a lot of people when they're drunk," Evelyn
Tremaine said. "He'd get on some subject and then he
wouldn't let go. He'd keep repeating himself, not knowing
that he was doing so, and when he got that way you couldn't
sidetrack him."

"Marion finally had enough," Choate added. "She said
she wanted to go, so we did. I think it was around midnight."

"And the accident," Standish said, glancing once more
at his report, "happened at one-ten. The insurance people
came to me afterward," he said, digressing easily. "Something to do with some policy having double indemnity. As
I remember, one contract was a personal policy and the
other had to do with your business." He glanced at Choate.
"Quite a sizable amount, wasn't it?"

"Two hundred thousand," Choate said. "On Robert's life
and on mine. We don't have a large operation and neither
of us is what you'd call wealthy. There was no double in-

demnity on that policy; just a straight business deal. After the accident the money went to the Tremaine estate and I took the business."

"The two hundred thousand came to you, Mrs. Tremaine?"

"Half of it," she said. "The other half went to Donald."

"And the personal insurance?" Standish asked, polite but still prodding.

"There were two policies totaling eighty thousand dollars and each had a double-indemnity clause. Robert's estate, if it ever gets out of probate, comes to me, but the insurance was just like the other policy—Donald and I shared it as joint beneficiaries."

"Why?"

The question came from Choate. It was direct and a little peremptory. In the back of his mind Standish had been expecting it and because he was still not quite sure how to make a simple answer he stalled.

"Why what, Mr. Choate?"

"Why are we here? What's this all about? Why are you rehashing something we would all like to forget?"

The entrance of Standish's secretary from the outer office saved him from an immediate answer and he eyed her with relief as she said:

"Dr. Tracey is on the line. I said you had some people with you but he thought you'd want to speak to him."

Standish thanked her, and excused himself as he picked up the telephone. When he said hello, Dr. Tracey wasted few words.

"You were right about the chloral hydrate. I doubt like hell if I would have known about it if I hadn't been looking for it. There are definite traces but not in any sizable amount. The drug, in itself, had nothing whatever to do with the man's death. I'll mail you a copy of my report. Okay?"

Standish racked the instrument slowly to give himself another second or two. There was no feeling of triumph or elation in learning that his hunch had been right, but as he prepared himself to answer Warren Choate the conviction remained that Ralph Estey had not killed Flemming.

"I'm not sure I can answer you," he said, "but I wonder if any of you happened to notice a piece in the morning paper about a man named Flemming who was shot to death in his apartment last night."

"I saw it," Choate said.

"So did I," Tremaine added.

"Did it occur to you that this might be the same man who killed Robert Tremaine?"

"It occurred to me," Choate said. "I figured it was the same guy. I decided that maybe there was some justice in the world after all."

"There was another piece in the afternoon paper," Donald Tremaine said. "According to this, the police are looking for Ralph Estey, the trumpet player who leads the band down at Hennessey's. They say he's wanted for questioning."

"And does this have something to do with us, Doctor?" Evelyn Tremaine asked.

"Probably not," Standish said. "But my autopsy report is not complete. That telephone call was from the pathologist at City Hospital. It looks very much as if Flemming was drugged before he was shot. I can't help wondering why."

He paused and thought: *Now take it easy, boy. Tread softly and don't say anything that could be considered actionable.*

"You see, the accident that happened to Robert Tremaine came up last night when I was discussing Flemming's death with Lieutenant Ballard. He thinks—and he's probably right —that any connection there would be coincidental. But he knows, and so does any experienced police officer, that hit-and-run fatalities are not always accidents. It's a method of murder that's been used before and will be used again because it's so hard to prove, particularly if a third party is involved."

He put up his hand to forestall some objection that Warren Choate seemed about to make and spoke quickly. "Same thing applies to some suicides. Medical examiners are aware of this; so are the police. What goes on the books as a fatal accident is sometimes a planned and deliberate suicide."

"But why—?"

Evelyn Tremaine had leaned forward, the dark eyes wide open and intent. Standish interrupted before she could finish.

"There could be several reasons. A person intent on killing himself will usually find a way. In the case of a man he may be thinking of an insurance policy with a suicide clause that would nullify the company's obligation. He may be thinking of his wife and children, of the publicity and possible disgrace. Checking into a man's emotional background and medical history sometimes provides a clue. But when that man runs into a utility pole, or a tree, or a stone wall at high speed it goes on the books as a traffic fatality. You'd be surprised at the number of accidents that happen while a man is all alone in a car."

He pushed back his chair and stood up, not wanting to say more, not wanting them to think too hard. Now that he realized that there was nothing more to learn here he wanted to get them out of the office before they started speculating or realized that his little dissertation was nothing more than an oblique cover-up for a more serious alternative. By the time they were on their feet, surprise and traces of bewilderment showing in their faces as they exchanged glances, he had already opened the door. He bowed slightly, smiled, and spoke politely as he said he hoped he had not inconvenienced them too much. He got rid of Donald Tremaine and his sister-in-law without difficulty but Choate stopped in the doorway, a scowl on his tan face and his muscular jaw set.

"I still don't know just what you're driving at, Doctor," he said. "You didn't actually say anything I could call you on but you made an inference or two—"

"I did?" Standish said as innocently as he could. "In what way?"

"You sounded as if you thought there might have been some collusion in Robert Tremaine's death."

"Was that your impression?" Standish sounded regretful and gave a small helpless shrug of his shoulders. "Then I'm afraid the conclusion is yours, not mine."

Choate seemed about to continue the discussion but something—it may have been Standish's polite and unperturbed expression, or the realization that further argument in his present frame of mind would be pointless—stopped him. He clamped his mouth shut and wheeled abruptly, the back of his neck pink.

As soon as Choate left the outer office, Standish knew what he wanted to do, and with his mind made up he had no intention of spoiling his decision with any rationalization of the impulse. His secretary already had her coat on and when she asked if there was anything more she could do he said no.

The telephone call he made when he was alone was to a private detective. His name was Lou Cheney and Standish had used him occasionally in the past when he needed outside help with an investigation. There was, in fact, an item in the city budget for just such expenses and heretofore the results that Cheney produced more than justified his fee. The detective's answering service said Cheney was out but that he was expected to call in shortly. Standish left his name and number but it was nearly seven o'clock before the call came and he heard the detective's voice.

"Lou," he said, "I've got a little job I'd like you to handle."

"Okay," Cheney said noncommittally. "Why don't you spell it out."

"It's got two parts," Standish said, and reminded the detective of the fatal accident.

"Yeah. I remember. Jess Flemming ran over a guy named Tremaine. . . . And, according to the papers, somebody walked in on Flemming last night and put a slug in his chest, right?"

"Right."

"They're looking for that trumpet player down at Hennessey's. Do you know if they found him yet?"

"Not that I know of. Have you got a pencil and a piece of paper? Write these names down."

"Warren Choate?" Cheney said when Standish gave him the name. "He's the one in the brokerage business that used to be a partner of the guy that got killed."

"He's separated from his wife," Standish said. "Her name is Marion. I understand there's a divorce in the works. Evelyn Tremaine is the widow and Donald Tremaine is the dead man's brother."

"So what about them?"

Standish said he'd like to find out what the four had been doing during the past several weeks, particularly in a social way.

"Who, of the opposite sex—if anyone—has Warren Choate, Evelyn, and Donald Tremaine been seeing lately? I'd like to know what they do with their spare time, especially in the evenings."

Even as he spoke Standish realized that he was asking quite a lot, and when there was no sound from the other end of the connection he wondered if Cheney was still there.

"Still on?"

"Sure. I was just thinking that this is kind of a funny business sometimes. I mean, sometimes one job will brush up against another. I should be able to help you a little because I've been doing some work along the same lines. I can't tell you who for or why. I'll have to think it over but I may be able to help. Is that all?"

Standish said no. "There was quite a bit of insurance involved in that accident." He mentioned the amounts and said: "The estate got two hundred thousand to be split between the brother and the wife, and Choate got the business. The other personal policies for eighty thousand carried double indemnity. They were divided like the other. I don't know about Robert Tremaine's personal estate but there must have been a will, because I understand it's still in probate. If it's a matter of record you should be able to find out how much it amounted to and who got it.

"I'm interested in bank accounts too," he said, and mentioned the date of Robert Tremaine's death. "Particularly during the period, say, a week before and a week after the accident."

Cheney, who had answered in grunts, found his voice.

"What am I?" he asked plaintively. "Houdini? You can't get bank records without a subpoena."

"I know that, but you've got a lot of friends around town. You should be able to get some sort of information confidentially if you give it the old Cheney try. Later, if anything comes up to make it official, we can get subpoenas. I don't expect miracles. Just do the best you can. One thing more. See what you can find out about Jess Flemming's financial status the last four months."

Cheney's reply was unenthusiastic. "I'll need some help," he said.

"Okay. Put another man on it with you."

Cheney grunted again. "It'll cost you a hundred bucks a day plus expenses."

"So?"

"So I was just wondering who was going to get it up—the city or you."

"Are you worried about it?"

"I don't know," Cheney said. "The only thing that bothers me is that you'll probably want all of it by nine o'clock tomorrow morning."

"Not by nine, Lou," Standish said, chuckling at the detective's reaction. "But sometime tomorrow and the sooner the better."

As soon as Standish broke the connection, he dialed his office number. Because of the time he expected to get the operator from his answering service and he was pleasantly surprised to hear Mary Hayward's voice.

"Hello, Mary. What are you doing there at this hour?"

"Trying to get some statements out." The voice was cool, businesslike, distant. "It's much easier when it's quiet around here."

"Well, good," Standish said. "Then why don't we have dinner?"

"I don't think so, thank you, Doctor. I have lamb chops in the icebox. I was just about to leave."

Standish recognized the impersonal tone. It was the sort of voice Mary employed when she did not entirely approve of him. She used it when Lieutenant Ballard made what she thought were unwarranted demands on the doctor's time; she used it when she thought he was neglecting his private practice or slighting wealthy patients who had wealthy friends. Because he understood her, the implied censure amused rather than annoyed Standish. For he was well aware that she also had in full measure the normal curiosity of any healthy young female and now he pursued his objective obliquely.

"Oh—I'm sorry," he said, making the words sound regretful. "In that case I guess we'll have to wait until tomorrow before I can tell you about this afternoon."

That brought a prolonged pause. He could almost see her thinking before she said: "This afternoon? You mean with those people you had me telephone? Did something happen?"

"Not really. Nothing of importance anyway. But I did
get an interesting call from Dr. Tracey over at City Hospital."

"The pathologist?"

"Yes. He ran some tests for me. It's beginning to look as
if someone may have administered some chloral hydrate—
what they used to call 'knockout drops'—to Flemming before he was shot last night, probably in the drink. . . . Are
you sure you won't change your mind about dinner?" he
added before she could reply.

She said: "Well—" and he knew he had her. There was a
momentary silence followed by an audible sigh. Then she
said, still with no great warmth: "How long will you be?"

"Fifteen minutes. Maybe less. You might get some ice
out. I could use a small drink."

9

MARY HAYWARD was waiting in Paul Standish's small
consulting room which connected the reception room and
the examining room at the rear. Her smooth young face,
perhaps deliberately, gave no indication of her mood but
she was no longer the efficient, white-uniformed girl the
office patients saw each day. She had changed to a simple
shirtwaist dress with buttons down most of the front and
a prim neckline, her medium-brown hair was softly waved,
and there was a trace of lipstick on her sweetly shaped
mouth.

"I got some ice out for you," she said as he took off his hat
and coat.

He said: "Thanks, Mary," and followed her into the examining room.

The refrigerator necessary for certain vaccines and medication held the customary ice trays and she had emptied one into a plastic bowl. She had taken a bottle of Scotch from a lower cabinet but there was only one glass. She drank very little as the usual thing but there were times, when they worked late, when she would join him while they discussed the day's affairs and interesting highlights in a friendly, congenial, and sometimes intimate way.

"None for you?" he said, holding the glass up.

"If we're going to eat out I'll have one then."

He poured whiskey, added ice and water. He took a grateful swallow, said "Ahh—" and steered her back to the more comfortable consulting room.

"Now," she said, settling herself in the patient's chair opposite the desk, "what's this about chloral hydrate? You said the man who was killed last night was shot."

"He was."

"So what made you think there was something else? What made you suspect he had taken anything?"

Standish told her, briefly but explicitly. He explained how he happened to find the "powder paper" and the suggestion he had made about it to Lieutenant Ballard.

"Ballard got a report from the city chemist that there actually was a trace of chloral hydrate in the paper. He argued —and he was right—that it could have been used earlier and not necessarily on Flemming."

"When did you hear from Dr. Tracey?"

"Just before I telephoned you from the morgue."

"And he said that Flemming actually took some chloral hydrate?"

"He certainly ingested it and the fact that it could be detected at all suggests that he took it not too long before he died."

He had Mary's full attention now. The well-spaced gray eyes were thoughtful and her growing frown was eroding her smooth brow.

"Would this have anything to do with the conference you had this afternoon?"

"I'm not sure. And until I knew about the chloral hydrate, one way or another, I couldn't quite accept the idea that Flemming's murder was as simple as it seemed."

"You mean you were suspicious."

"A little, I guess."

"And when you get that way you won't give up."

Standish grinned at her, knowing what she meant. In his own defense he said: "I can't help thinking what Doc Lathrop used to keep telling me."

"Yes," Mary said and sighed resignedly. " 'The truth always rings true.' What's the rest of it?"

" 'But the appearance of truth varies widely.' . . . Jess Flemming killed Robert Tremaine."

"Accidentally."

"On the face of it, yes."

"If it hadn't been for the discarded paper with the traces of chloral hydrate you would have accepted the police theory that Ralph Estey, or some other enemy of Flemming's, had walked in and shot him."

"Yes."

"But now you're suggesting that the Tremaine accident was not an accident, that someone hired Flemming to run Tremaine down as part of some plot."

"Not suggesting, Mary. Just wondering—"

The telephone's shrill summons saved him from further argument and Mary glowered at it before she snatched it up.

"Dr. Standish's office."

He could see the sudden tightening of her face as some reply came to her, heard her say: "Yes, he's here, Lieutenant. Why do you want him? Don't tell me you've found another body? . . . What? . . . All right, all right," she added irritably. "Here he is."

She handed over the telephone, her voice quietly furious. "Oh, damn. He would call now."

"Doc?" Ballard said, wasting no time on the amenities. "Got a job for you. Do you want to drive or do I send a car?"

"I'll drive. Where?"

"Hennessey's."

"What?"

"I'll have a man out front to tell you where to go. Make it soon, hunh?"

Standish heard the click in his ear before he could reply. He replaced the instrument slowly, not daring to look at Mary, and, for one of the few times, sharing fully her views on the duties and obligations and drawbacks of serving as medical examiner.

"I'm sorry," he said, still not looking at her.

"Oh, that's all right," she said stiffly. "This sort of thing is to be expected, isn't it? Who is it this time?"

"He didn't say."

"Where?"

"Hennessey's. . . . And look," he added earnestly, "we can still have dinner. Come with me and—"

"No, thank you."

"You can order drinks for us. I probably won't be long and—"

Again she interrupted and when he saw the set expression around the mouth and the distant and detached look in the gray eyes he gave up.

"The lamb chops are still in the icebox," she said, reaching for her camel's-hair coat. "I should have insisted on cooking them in the first place." She got as far as the door and then did an about-face.

"I'm sorry," she said, a sudden contriteness in her voice and an odd mistiness in her eyes. "I don't know why I have to make it worse for you. It's just that I wish you didn't have to—oh, never mind." She straightened her shoulders and stuck her chin out. "Be sure and give the lieutenant my best regards."

There was an unmarked police car in front of Hennessey's and another with the city's insignia on the door across the street as Paul Standish bumped his sedan into the parking lot. He crossed the street diagonally, bag in hand, and a plainclothesman stepped out of the shadows to meet him.

"No ambulance yet?"

"In the alley out back. Hennessey is about to have a stroke and the lieutenant wants to humor him. You know, all those people eating dinner and Hennessey afraid they'll walk out. Let me have your bag. I'll go around. Keep on straight through the left-hand doorway next to the bandstand and I'll meet you there."

Standish watched the man go and stood a moment at the curb, his back to the entrance. For the next few seconds there was no traffic and the street was quiet. Overhead the night sky was clear and star-studded, the silhouette of rooftops well defined. He saw all this and heard the city noises from other blocks but none of this registered. On the short drive from his office he had tried to keep his imagination in check but now that he was here a strange sort of fear was working on him and he felt a sense of foreboding and uncertainty as he turned and entered the restaurant.

His pace was deliberate as he removed his hat, and as he passed the checkroom there was no smiling Sheila Keith to greet him. Behind the counter was a youth that he identified as a bus boy, apparently pressed into service, and this knowledge served to increase his fears. The dining area seemed to be about half full. There were six or eight men at the bar who watched him pass. The most noticeable feature was the strange stillness that seemed to descend upon the room, the lack of conversation.

He felt other eyes upon him as he skirted the tiny dance floor and continued past the empty bandstand. He pushed the curtain aside and now he saw three members of the orchestra talking in hushed tones, cigarettes in hand. They were leaning against the wall opposite the stairs. They nodded silently, eyes averted, and the detective with the doctor's bag came to meet him from the rear.

"Upstairs, Doc," he said.

The door of the first of the two upstairs rooms stood open and white light from the police photographer's flood lamps spilled into the hall. These same lamps kept Standish from a detailed inspection of the interior but when the photographer noticed him and snapped them off he was only vaguely aware of Lieutenant Ballard and Captain Cavanaugh and the sparsely furnished dusty room.

Instead his eyes went directly to the oddly bent figure on the floor beside the overturned chair and partly obscured by the table. He could tell from there that it was a man and now the doubt in his mind vanished and he could feel an insidious sickness working on his stomach. For although his profession made him a spectator to death in almost all its violent forms, he had never, as a medical examiner, been called on to inspect the body of anyone he personally knew and admired.

Moving slowly as he rounded the table, and trying to block out all emotional considerations, he saw first the small ugly hole in Ralph Estey's head just in front of the right ear, the blackened rim surrounding it. The slight still figure was lying partly on its side, and after his first, all-inclusive look Standish put down his bag, glanced impersonally at Ballard and the grizzled, cigar-chewing face of Captain Cavanaugh, who was first to speak.

"We're making it easy for you these days, Doc. You won't have to do much lab work on this one either. Just give us some idea when he pulled the trigger."

Standish paid no attention to the remarks. He saw again the discarded copies of *Variety* and *Downbeat*, the dog-eared pack of playing cards. He saw the pint bottle of bour-

D

bon on the table and noted that it was more empty than
full. He put his coat and hat on the shabby couch and took
out his notebook as Dr. Lathrop's training made itself felt.
He started to sketch the scene. He said:

"Who found him?"

"The piano player," Cavanaugh said. "And you know why
it took so long?"

Standish had a pretty good idea but to keep Cavanaugh
occupied he said: "No. Why?"

"They call this the musicians' room," Cavanaugh said, his
tone disparaging. "It's off limits to everybody but the band.
Even Hennessey. Just like they got a closed corporation.
Mondays a cleaning woman gives it a weekly going over.
Monday night—last night—the joint is closed. Today nobody looks because unless Estey calls a rehearsal nobody's
ever here until evening anyway. Tonight the piano player
comes in a little early—about eight o'clock—and finds him.
He runs for Hennessey and Hennessey has a fit. He knows
he has to call in no matter how much business he's doing
but he makes it a personal call to Ballard and asks him to
take it easy. . . . So what do you think?"

Standish had righted the overturned straight-backed
chair and now he eased down and began to test the body
for signs of *rigor mortis*. Just as with Jess Flemming the
night before, he started first to determine the condition of
the jaw and neck. He moved slowly downward through
arms, torso, legs, and feet because the disappearance of
rigor occurred in the same order as its onset. When he finished he glanced at the other side of the head and looked
up at Cavanaugh.

"What do you want from me?"

"How long has he been dead?"

"I can't tell you from the condition of *rigor* alone. It varies
in individuals. It makes a difference whether the person
died during a struggle or in bed. Powerfully built men de-
velop it slowly and retain it longer—"

"Estey was no muscle man."

"It normally persists for from twelve to forty-eight hours. There's still some *rigor* here," Standish said as though he had not heard.

"His watch is run down," Ballard said. "If he wound it at night, I mean as a usual thing, then he died before he had a chance to wind it."

"Come on, Doc," Cavanaugh said. "We don't want a lecture about chemical changes and the reason for *rigor*. I've heard it before. All we want is some help. Give us a guess, will you?"

"Off the record?"

"Any way."

"Twenty-four hours. Give or take six hours. If you expect me to put it any closer than that find out when he ate last, and where, and what."

"We can give it a try," Ballard said. "For now we'll have to assume that it happened sometime last night."

"If you're still hanging on to the theory on Jess Flemming," Standish said, "you can put it a little closer, can't you?"

Ballard nodded but Cavanaugh was not quite so quick.

"How do you mean?" he demanded.

"Flemming was apparently shot between eight and ten. If Estey is your man and *if he killed himself* he must have done so afterward."

"Sure. How else could it be?"

Cavanaugh buttoned his topcoat and settled his hat. He took the dead cigar from his mouth, brushed off the ashes, and relit it. When he had it drawing to his satisfaction he blew smoke at Standish.

"Okay, Doc. He's all yours. Unless the lieutenant has some new ideas, which I doubt like hell. . . . See you." . . .

When Standish had ordered the body removed he sat down on the couch, his expression somber and a look of discouragement in his dark-blue eyes. The inner sickness was no longer with him but his depression continued. He made a conscious effort to brush aside the mental fatigue that had begun to cloud his thoughts. When his glance touched the pint bottle on the table he asked if Ballard was going to check it for prints.

"Sure," Ballard said. "It's part of the routine."

"What about the gun?"

"It was right beside him. We're checking that too, not that it ever does much good. I never found any prints on a gun yet that were worth a damn. But it was a .32 with two empty shells. We also got the slug." Ballard went over and sat in the chair next to the table. "We figure he was sitting here when he pulled the trigger. The bullet went through his head almost horizontally and buried itself a little ways in the plaster, which is a break because it will mean it's in good enough shape for our ballistics man to check with the one you found in Jess Flemming."

He pointed to a white scar in the yellowish calcimined wall where someone had extracted the bullet.

"From what I could see," Standish said, "I doubt if it was a contact wound. When I shave these sideburns I'll know for sure."

"But it was close."

"Not more than two inches, I'd say."

"Is there anything about that that's inconsistent with suicide?"

"No," Standish said, and as his thoughts moved on, he added: "There wasn't any drinking glass, was there?"

"No glass," Ballard said, "but do you know a quicker way to get drunk than taking it right from the bottle?"

"You have a point. So how do you figure it?"

Ballard tipped his head, his gray gaze curious. "Is there more than one way?"

"I'd like to hear you say it out loud. But before you start— have you heard from Dr. Tracey?"

"I got a call from him around six but no report yet."

"What did he say about chloral hydrate?"

"He said Flemming had some in his system, probably taken not too long before he died."

"Okay." Standish leaned back and reached for a cigarette. "I'm listening."

"I think Estey walked in on Flemming last night with a gun and used it. I'm not going to try and guess about the chloral hydrate because I think it's incidental. There could be several ways to account for it. Somebody else could have slipped him the drug; maybe that Keith girl. But however Flemming got it I think Estey did the job. It's the only way it adds up. If he had guts enough to tackle Flemming with his fists Friday night he had enough to use the gun."

"It's not the same thing. If Estey had had a gun Friday I agree he might have used it. But this other was cold-blooded and premeditated."

"Because that Friday-night business had been eating away at him," Ballard argued. "He probably brooded about it until he couldn't stand it. He made a threat, said he had a gun. When it got too much for him he used it."

"I don't think so."

"As a medical man or—"

"Leave out the adjective. I knew Estey pretty well. I'll even agree that nearly everyone can kill given the proper provocation and the right set of circumstances."

He paused, his mind slipping back to his Friday-night talk with the trumpet player, remembering not only the mention of the gun but the statement that if Estey couldn't run fast enough he'd use it on himself. He saw no point in mentioning it now but he still could not quite accept it as more than the exaggerated statement of a discouraged and recently humiliated man.

"You think he shot Flemming, lost his courage, got to brooding, bought a bottle—" He stopped as a new thought came to him. "How could he get in here last night?"

"He had a key," Ballard said. "The band rehearsed some-times during the day when the place wasn't open. And I go along with what you were saying. When Estey had a chance to think, he knew he was a dead duck anyway. He had no place to go. He knew we wouldn't know about this room, that he'd be safe here for a while. But he also knew that we'd grab him in a day or two, knew we'd find out about the fight, and the threat he made. He brought a bot-tle in here with him and started hitting it. The more he drank, the more he brooded. When he realized the score, when the despair or hopelessness or whatever you want to call it got too much for him, he had enough false courage to pull the trigger. How else can you figure it?"

It was an articulate and sincere statement and Standish lacked the facts to argue the alternatives. He was not con-vinced but he understood that his reluctance to accept the explanation was a matter of personal judgment and preju-dice, which had as its basis no more than his own feelings about the victim.

"You could be right, Tom," he said, "but, knowing Estey, I can't quite buy that yet." He put out his cigarette and leaned forward on the couch. "Will you do me a favor?"

Ballard eyed him with veiled suspicion before he said: "If I can."

"I don't have to hurry the p.m., so have your lab man do a paraffin test on Estey's right hand sometime tonight, will you?"

"A paraffin test?" Ballard's tone was openly incredulous. "You have to be kidding. That test is old-hat these days."

"So I've heard."

"It's not conclusive. It won't stand up in court."

"I know."

"It's a fact," Ballard said, trying to be patient, "that no hand gun has an absolutely tight breech. They discovered years ago that there could be traces of nitrate, or whatever the hell they make powder of, on a man's hand when he

fired a gun. Twenty years ago nobody argued the point until some smart guy discovered that there were other ways of
getting the same characteristic traces on the hand of a man
who never even had a gun."

"Sure," Standish said, and grinned at the vehemence of
the lieutenant's argument.

"What do you mean, sure? What's your point?"

"Well, if your paraffin test comes up with those characteristic traces you speak of you have done me a favor. If,
on the other hand, Estey's hand happens to be clean then
you'd better look around for some explanation of how he
could put that bullet through his brain without holding a
gun."

Ballard started to say something and then stopped. He
scowled at Standish, annoyance showing in his gray eyes.
He stalked across the room and came back. He stepped
into a tiny cubicle that contained a toilet, a washbowl, and
two smudged and dirty glasses that had not seen soap and
hot water in weeks. He removed his hat and replaced it.
He grunted and gave a tiny shake of his head before he digressed.

"What is it with you anyway, Doc? Anybody'd think this
guy was your brother."

"Will you have the test made?"

"Well—sure. But if you think it's going to prove—"

"I'm not talking about proof in the literal sense," Standish
said, interrupting. "I'd just like to get at the truth. I'm going
to keep digging until I do. . . . What about Sheila Keith?"
he asked, to change the subject.

"How do you mean?" Ballard said, the scowl still working
on his good-looking face.

"She knows about this, doesn't she?"

"Sure. It shook her pretty bad."

"There was a bus boy in the checkroom when I came in."

"We got her into the ladies' lounge without too much fuss
and I sent for a policewoman. She's with her now. I told

her I'd have to talk to her in a little while. I wanted to get
rid of the body first, so we might as well have her in here
now."

10

TO ALL who did not know her, Sheila Keith might have
looked like any other attractive young woman with ash-
blond hair and a trim, well-molded figure. She had her chin
up and her stride was steady when she came in with the
policewoman at her side, but Standish saw the unaccus-
tomed pallor in the high-cheekboned face and the strained,
set lines about the mouth. The mascara and eye shadow
were messy now and the lipstick uneven. She had been cry-
ing and the green eyes were still bright with unwanted
tears.

Ballard indicated a chair and asked her to sit down in a
voice that was considerate and a little embarrassed. He
nodded to the policewoman, a sturdy girl in a gray-woolen
suit and small felt hat. Plain-looking but not unattractive,
she could have passed as anyone's thirty-five-year-old secretary, and Ballard, calling her simply Murphy, asked her to
wait in the hall.

"We won't be long. You can see that Miss Keith gets home
when we finish." He sat on the edge of the couch next to
Standish and looked at Sheila Keith. "Are you all right
now?"

"I'm fine," she said, unable to control her bitterness. "Just
fine."

Ballard eyed Standish aslant, raising and then lowering
his brows before he continued to the girl.

"You know what happened here?"

"I know what your Sergeant Cooney told me but I don't believe it. Not for one minute."

"You mean you don't believe he committed suicide?"

"Not any more than I ever believed he shot Jess Flemming. He wasn't that kind of man." She looked right at Standish, an undertone of desperation in her words. "Could he, Doctor? You knew him. You were a friend of his; he spoke of you often. Do you think he did this thing?"

"No," Standish said, "but unfortunately that's only my personal opinion."

"Yesterday," she continued as though she had not been listening, "I thought it was all my fault." She looked at Ballard. "I told the doctor so."

"Your fault? How do you mean?"

"Well, you were so sure Ralph did it, and nobody could find him, and so I thought maybe he *did* shoot Flemming. And if that was so, it had to be my fault. I knew what Flemming was like," she added, and went on to repeat some of the things she had told Standish that morning, using all the uncomplimentary adjectives she could think of.

"I wasn't really in love with Ralph," she said. "I wasn't thinking about marrying him, not the way things were. If I had just pretended I didn't want to be bothered and stopped seeing him there wouldn't have been any fight Friday night. But I liked Ralph. We had a lot in common. He was considerate and thoughtful and a very understanding guy. I never led him on or built up any hopes but I didn't exactly discourage him either. Now I don't think I had anything to do with it. I mean, except for that fight Friday night."

"I don't happen to agree with you," Ballard said quietly. "But for now, assuming that you're right, that would mean that someone, identity unknown, walked in on Jess Flemming last night and shot him."

"And why not? The kind of man he was there must be dozens of people who would like to see him dead."

"Then there wouldn't be any reason for Estey's committing suicide, would there?" Ballard said.

"No. That's what I'm telling you."

"Which would mean that someone else did a very clever job and set it up to make it look exactly like a suicide."

The thought stopped her for a moment. Tiny furrows warped her brow. She glanced at Standish as though looking for some assistance; then back at Ballard.

"Well, yes. I suppose so."

"We recovered both bullets," Ballard said. "One last night, one tonight. Both are .32 caliber. By morning we'll know if they were fired from the same gun. If they were—and I'll gamble on it—then that means that the same unknown person did both jobs."

"Well"—the painted mouth twisted slightly and she swallowed visibly—"couldn't it have happened that way?"

"Not unless you can give us the name of someone who hated Ralph Estey enough to kill him. On Flemming, we might come up with something—"

"Nobody hated Ralph," she said, giving Ballard no chance to finish. "Everybody liked him."

"Maybe so." Ballard gestured with one hand. "But if we're going to get anywhere on your theory, we'll need some help. You were pretty close to him, so do some thinking. If you get any ideas, let us know."

The red mouth grew crooked and her tone became accusing. "But you don't believe it, do you? Not any part of it."

"As of now, no." Ballard stood up to signal the end of the interview. She rose, still watching him, and he moved with her toward the door. "Are you sure Estey didn't try to get in touch with you last night or early today?"

"Positive. I didn't talk with him, I didn't see him."

Ballard said "All right" as he opened the door. He asked her to keep thinking, adding that if she came up with anything he'd like to hear about it. When he came back to Standish he took a big breath and exhaled noisily. His small grin was wry, so was his voice when he spoke.

"She's a hard dame to convince." He considered the statement and the grin remained. "And so are you. . . . Don't tell me," he added quickly to forestall a reply. "I know. All you want is the truth. You want a favor on the paraffin test and I'll go along with you there. How about doing me one?"

"Sure." Standish reached for his hat and coat. "What do you have in mind?"

"Nobody's been out to tell Estey's ex-wife about this and it looks like I'm elected. You were a friend of his. Did you ever meet her?"

"A couple of times, as I remember," Standish said. "This was two or three years ago, before they separated. . . . She knows you were looking for Estey, doesn't she?"

"Sure. Cooney talked to her. She didn't know anything. We kept the house staked out, just in case. The husband— the name is Johnson now—is a toolmaker. He's got a pretty good job."

"There's also a five-year-old boy."

"Yeah," Ballard said. "I don't think it'll be too sticky but I could use a little of your moral support. It's only about a twenty-minute ride. Okay?"

"Sure. If you'll spring for a drink when we finish."

Ballard grinned and squeezed Standish's shoulder. He said it was a deal.

The Johnson home was a modest ranch-style dwelling in a new development of similar houses not far from the Thruway. Painted white and standing rather close to the street, it had a screened-in porch on one side and an attached garage on the other close by the property line. The door of this was open and empty, and Ballard, spotting this as he stopped beyond the drive, said: "If the husband is out it will be easier. . . . You say you've met her?"

"What you mean is," Standish said, "will I lead the way?"

"Yeah. You get us in and I'll do the talking."

There was a light on behind drawn curtains on the right, and a few seconds after Standish rang another light popped on over the front door. They stood on the square concrete slab which made the second of two steps while a woman's face appeared in the diamond-shaped glass in the upper part of the door. Presently a latch clicked and the door opened on a chain.

Standish took off his hat and said: "Good evening, Mrs. Johnson. I'm Dr. Standish. We met a couple of years ago when—"

"Oh, yes." The chain was removed and the opening widened. "You're a friend of Ralph's. Is—is that why you're here? Did they find him?"

"This is Lieutenant Ballard of the city police. Yes, they found him. The lieutenant would like to talk to you. May we come in?"

She moved backward with some reluctance. "I don't know how I can help. My husband's bowling. He should be back in another half hour or so—"

Her voice trailed off and she backed into the center of the rectangular room, a pleasant-faced woman in a neat blue-and-white-print house dress. She looked to be in her early thirties, with dark hair and eyes, a nice complexion, and, at the moment, a nervous, harried manner. She backed to a sofa upholstered to match two overstuffed chairs. She sat down gingerly, knees together and hands folded in her lap while Ballard cleared his throat.

"Where?" she asked before he could speak. "Where was he hiding?"

"Do you know the room upstairs in the back of Hennessey's? What they call the musicians' room?"

"I've heard Ralph speak of it." Her eyes opened and things happened behind them. "He was there all this time?"

"The piano player found him around eight tonight. He was dead, Mrs. Johnson. According to Dr. Standish, probably for twenty-four hours or so. He'd been shot in the temple. The way it looks it was suicide. I'm sorry."

She caught her breath quickly and the fabric of the print dress tightened across her breasts. She said: "Oh, no!" and her hands flew to the sides of her face. For a second or so the shock and bewilderment of the announcement took charge of her features and then some inner effort to keep her self-control won out over the emotional impact.

"Killed himself? Ralph?" The hands slid limply down from her cheeks. "I don't believe it. Why?"

"Because we think he shot Jess Flemming last night," Ballard said, and went on quickly to state the official position.

Standish, no longer listening to the familiar arguments, glanced around the comfortable but ordinary room. He found himself wondering about Mr. Johnson and Estey's five-year-old son, and what effect this would have on his life. He remembered the insurance policy Estey had spoken of and now, as if by some magic of telepathy, he heard the woman open the subject.

"We can get along without the twenty-five a week Ralph was supposed to pay for Billy's support," she said, her mouth pinched and a strained, closed look on her face. "My husband makes a good living. But I counted on that insurance policy."

"What policy is that, Mrs. Johnson?" Ballard said.

"For ten thousand dollars. It was to be for Billy's education. It was part of the divorce settlement. It had a suicide clause for the first two years and it wasn't nearly that long. Now Billy will get nothing. But Ralph would never think of that."

She stopped and again something happened to her face. The pinched look had gone and a slackness came and now the lower lip trembled and the eyes filled.

"I don't mean that," she said, her voice shaking. "I shouldn't talk like that. We had some good times at first, some wonderful times. Ralph was working regularly and cutting records right and left. Never for himself. He'd never push hard enough for that, but other band leaders would ask him to sit in. I still have most of them. Those old records, I mean. I didn't mind the hotel rooms and the small apartments and the traveling. I never played an instrument but I enjoyed being around the band and Ralph said I had a good ear.

"It was different after Billy came. Ralph could have settled down. He had lots of talent and good offers and he was a fine arranger. He could have made it with a studio band and from what I've heard once you do you're set. If you behave yourself you have a steady spot and good money and you can live like other people instead of moving from one job to another and never getting more than a few dollars ahead."

She swallowed and said: "I guess with Ralph his trumpet came first. He used to quote something that Louis Armstrong once told him. Something about having to give more time to the brass than to the piano or the drums or the reeds or the strings. He said if you were going to blow that instrument right, you had to devote your life to it.

"I came from this part of the state," she added, "and when we came back here and I saw Ralph was never going to change I couldn't take it any longer. He had ability but he wouldn't compromise. It was as if things finally caught up with him and there was no way to go but down. I still don't believe he killed that man Flemming. I can't figure why he should, but then I never really could figure Ralph."

She stopped abruptly, as though aware of her voice for the first time. Tears glistened on her cheeks now as memories of happier times broke down her defenses. She made a loud sniffing sound, came quickly to her feet, and almost ran to a table near the door. When she had opened her handbag and found a handkerchief she blew hard, her back to them. She wiped her eyes before she turned.

"What do you want from me?" she demanded. "What can I tell you that I didn't tell that detective that came here this morning to question me?"

"What did he want to know, Mrs. Johnson?" Ballard asked gently.

"He wanted to know if I'd seen Ralph lately and I told him no. He said didn't I ever see him, and I said before Ralph started those Sunday-afternoon jazz concerts he used to come every other week and take Billy for a ride." Again she dug at her eyes with the wadded handkerchief. "What am I going to tell Billy?"

The sound of the muffled, desolate voice that expected no answer brought a growing thickness to Standish's throat. He felt hot and uncomfortable and helpless. Now he nudged Ballard and gestured toward the door with a small jerk of his head.

"Billy's young, Mrs. Johnson," he said. "He doesn't read the newspapers. All he has to know is that his father has gone away on a trip."

"We went over Estey's hotel room pretty thoroughly," Ballard said. "We couldn't find anything that would tell us whether he had any relatives or not. Would you know about that?"

She stood straighter now, hands at her sides and clenched but not rigid. "He had a married sister out West somewhere. I might have her address. Do I have to get it now?"

"In the morning will do," Ballard said. "Someone will have to notify her. Think about it. Maybe discuss it with your husband." He followed Standish to the door. "Someone will call you in the morning. You can let us know what you want to do."

I I

ON WEDNESDAY, Paul Standish was again forced to have his sandwich and milk at his desk. He had met Dr. Emerson at the morgue at seven and the autopsy had been routine, showing nothing significant except the head wound. He had told Mary Hayward about Estey, keeping his account as brief as possible and listening absently to her shocked and bewildered comments. He had made four house calls and now, his sandwich finished and Mary out to lunch with friends, he called police headquarters and asked for Lieutenant Ballard.

"Anything new?"

"No," said Ballard, and he did not elaborate. "What did your p.m. show?"

"Just what you thought it would show."

"No complications?"

"No."

"No chloral hydrate?" The question was mildly sardonic and needed no answer.

"Did you have your man make the paraffin test on Estey's right hand?"

"I did."

"Well?"

"Well what?"

"How did the test come out?"

"Negative."

"Ahh—"

"It's still not conclusive."

"You're a stubborn man."

"And a practical one," Ballard countered. "From the physical facts—and until we have something conclusive that says otherwise—the official position is suicide. The State's Attor-

ney will go along. If you want to disagree and would like to
say so to the press, it will be your neck, not mine."

"Fair enough. Fortunately the press hasn't bothered me,
but personally and privately and for your ears only, I'll take
the minority view."

He glanced again at his appointment book when Mary
returned and told her not to make any after-hours appointments that afternoon. She did not argue but her disapproval
was apparent in her face and in her tone as she said: "Very
well, Doctor."

For once he was able to keep to schedule. There were
no complications, no emergency calls, and few complaints.
As a result the office was empty by three-twenty. As soon as
the door closed Standish reached for his hat and coat.

"I don't know how long I'll be gone, Mary," he said. "You
can run along whenever you're ready."

"But—where can I reach you?"

"I can't tell you that either," he said, avoiding her glance.
"When you leave tell the answering service I'll be in touch
when I can. If anything comes up that can't wait they'll
have to call in someone else." He turned at the door and,
seeing the disturbed and reproachful look in her gray eyes,
he added: "It shouldn't be more than an hour or two."

The address Standish sought was only three blocks away,
a modest apartment house in a quiet neighborhood that was
considered more upper-middle-class than fashionable. The
name plates in the foyer told him that Marion Choate had
apartment 3-B and he rode up in the automatic elevator
trying to think of some reasonable opening remark.

The woman who opened the door in response to his ring
had a lot of auburn hair, hazel eyes, and a sturdy, full-
fashioned figure. She wore a plain gray skirt and a white
blouse transparent enough to show the well-filled brassière
underneath. The eyes under the heavy but well-shaped
brows looked right at him in that first second and revealed
nothing.

"Yes?"

"Mrs. Choate?" Standish, still with no worthwhile gambit, gave her one of his bedside-manner smiles. "I'm Dr. Standish."

"Oh?" The eyes were at once observant and showed humorous glints. "M.D. or Ph.D?"

The remark broke the ice for Standish and his grin became more genuine. "M.D., Mrs. Choate. As a matter of fact I'm the medical examiner. I saw you with your husband at the hearing last December when Robert Tremaine was killed. I tried to get in touch with you yesterday—"

"Yes, I know. Warren called this morning and told me you talked to the others. I was in New York for the day." There was somehow a look of approval in her smile now as she stepped back. "Come in. Come in. . . . Is it too early for a drink?"

Standish, a little uncertain about such sudden hospitality, mumbled a reply by saying: "A little, I'm afraid. I mean, for me."

"Yes. I suppose a doctor has to be careful but I'm sure you won't object if I have one." She started to turn away; then turned and smiled again.

"I don't see your doctor's bag, and there's no stethoscope around your neck, so I gather that this is not a professional call but a social one."

Standish bowed his head to hide an incipient grin. It was about all he could do under the circumstances. But the delay, while she went to a well-supplied sidebar and poured Scotch over the three ice cubes she had put into a glass, gave him a chance to regroup mentally. It was a nice room, not elaborate but with wall-to-wall carpeting and well-chosen pieces.

"Well," she said coming toward him with the drink in her hand. "Just what brought you here, Doctor? Something to do with that accident last December?"

"Yes," Standish said, still a little uncomfortable in this woman's presence but feeling the warmth of her greeting and offhand manner. "Sort of cleaning up some loose ends."

By then he was well aware of her full hips and breasts. In later years, without proper dieting, she might be heavy, but the full mouth and short upper lip, the frank inspection of her eyes, suggested a sensual appetite not easily satisfied. When she sat down on the divan and motioned to a place beside her he took it but kept a good three feet between them.

"Your husband said that you are separated," he said, "and that a divorce is in the works."

"Correct on both counts."

"And you—by that I mean you and your husband—have been friendly with the Tremaines. I mean, when Mr. Tremaine was alive—"

He let the sentence go because he realized that he was talking like a college freshman. He made a mental effort to pull himself together. The woman was not flirting with him in the accepted sense of the word but she had somehow put him on the defensive and it was not a comfortable feeling. He decided to concentrate, to level, to stop beating about the bush.

"I'm right about that, am I not?"

"Indeed you are. Robert and Warren were in school together. The business, such as it is, was started by Robert's father. Warren was one of the hired help, one of the bright ones, I might add. So when Mr. Tremaine, senior, died it was natural enough for them to try and run the business together."

"I see," Standish said, still not satisfied with his progress. "I know about the business insurance policy and I assume that now, being sole owner of the business, your husband is a little better off financially than he was before the accident."

"True." She sipped her drink and crossed her legs. She

watched him with good humor but also with some obvious speculation.

"Which could mean, for instance, that your husband's alimony settlement will be more acceptable to you than it might have been, shall we say, last November before the accident. In other words—"

"In other words, yes." She took some more of her drink and began to wiggle her low-heeled shoe up and down on the crossed foot. "Warren wants a divorce, and so do I. We were married ten years, roughly, and I entered the holy state of matrimony at twenty-two. So now you know how old I am."

"And that foursome of yours," Standish said, beginning to like what he was doing, "developed into a situation where you could see that your husband and Evelyn Tremaine were somewhat sympatico."

She laughed abruptly but the sound was genuine. She took another swallow of her drink. She flipped the heel of her loosely fastened shoe up and down again.

"I like you, Doctor," she said, and there was no doubt in Standish's mind that she meant it. "Sympatico?" She savored the word. "Indeed yes."

She finished her drink and put the glass down, and suddenly she was no longer smiling and the change in her mood was obvious.

"I'll level with you, Doctor. Warren and I haven't had anything going for quite some time. In the beginning we both did not want children too soon. We wanted fun. We wanted to roll around in the sack to our hearts' content—forgive the phrase—without obligations. So time went by, as time does. Warren said no kids, at least for now, et cetera, et cetera. Well I do. I want them before I get too old to have them. I also discovered that Warren by himself was not quite enough any more. He has a girl and I found a man who thinks a little more my way. In New York. Everything is coming up roses—where did I hear that?—so now you have a capsule account of our marital life."

"And the night of the accident," Standish said, focusing his mind on the subject that had brought him here, "you and your husband had a bit of a tiff—for one reason or another—with Robert and Evelyn Tremaine. You left before they did."

"Right," she said emphatically. "We left. Never mind why or who said 'Let's go.'"

"Your husband brought you home?"

"He did."

"And you undressed and went to bed."

"I did. He, fed up to here with his darling wife, said: 'I'll see you, toots,' and took off."

"For where?"

"'To get another drink and get away from you,' to quote him."

"Do you know what time he came back?"

"I do not." She waved one hand in the general direction of the hall. "We have two bedrooms here—his and hers. I have no objection to normal and frequent man-woman relationships in marriage. In fact I highly recommend them. But for me Warren wasn't the man and hadn't been for some time."

"Then, except for Robert Tremaine, who apparently was too drunk to know what hit him, the accident made it a little easier for the rest of you, at least in some respects."

"I suppose you could look at it that way. Warren is certainly somewhat more affluent than he was."

"From what you say Evelyn Tremaine was no longer particularly in love with her husband at the time."

"I think you could say that."

"She also received half of the company insurance, half of the personal policies that have double-indemnity clauses in them. There also must have been some personal estate of her husband's. Would you know how much that amounted to?"

"I may have heard Warren mention it. I wouldn't want to be quoted but I seem to remember that it might run around a hundred thousand after taxes."

"That should be enough to make her a rather desirable catch."

"If you happen to like your woman thin and cold and snooty-looking."

"What about Donald Tremaine?" Standish asked, hoping he could keep her talking.

"How do you mean?"

"Well—he benefited financially as much as anyone when his brother was killed, didn't he?"

"Indeed he did. Until then he'd been a mousy little book-keeper making maybe eight thousand a year. I understand he took the hundred thousand he got as his half of the company insurance and bought himself a partnership in the firm he'd been working for. I understand he's a vice-president now. I think Warren said he should take down close to twenty thousand a year from now on if you include his share of the profits."

"You didn't know him well? In a personal way?"

"No. I'm afraid I can't help you much there. Our paths seldom crossed. Donald always seemed a little too proper and fastidious and moody and straight-laced and naïve. Evelyn could probably tell you more if you want to bother to ask her."

She turned toward him, her arm across the back of the divan now and bringing up one knee on the cushions. The hazel eyes still held the humorous, speculative glints and he had the idea she was mocking him just a little as she said:

"Does this take care of the loose ends you mentioned when you came, Doctor?"

"You've been very helpful."

"And just what is it you're trying to prove?"

Standish had no ready answer but he did the best he could. He mentioned the Flemming murder and spoke of Ralph Estey.

"I'm beginning to wonder," he said guardedly, "whether that accident that killed Robert Tremaine was as simple as it seemed."

"What else could it have been?"

"There's a possibility that it could have been planned that way."

The hazel eyes were no longer smiling but wide open and concerned.

"You mean it was deliberate? That someone hired this man Flemming?"

"I think it's possible."

"And what do the police think?"

"They don't agree."

He stood up, deciding he had gone as far as he could. She uncurled her legs and came to her feet as he started toward the door. He turned there and found her standing close. She did not seem to be upset and she was studying him again, the eyes appraising. When she leaned forward another inch he could feel the points of her breasts touch the front of his jacket. She did not seem to notice this; neither did she move and he felt again the physical pull of this woman's body and personality. He understood without conscious thought that this was one—if she liked you—who would not lie flat on her back with her hands quietly at her sides. He shook his head to dispel the image because there was another woman he had to talk to and he wanted to approach her with an open mind.

He thanked her for her help and she gave him her hand as she stepped back, the pressure of her fingers firm and lingering.

"Any time, Doctor." The smile was back. "Any time at all.

Maybe next time the hour will be late enough to have a drink with me."

I 2

EVELYN TREMAINE lived fairly close to Marion Choate's apartment but the neighborhood itself seemed far removed. No business establishments or apartment buildings had encroached on this area of old homes and well-kept lawns and quiet streets. The house he sought was a brick colonial of two stories and attic, not large but substantial, with wall chimneys on each side, a white-trimmed door, and a handsome fanlight.

It was several seconds after Paul Standish had pushed the bell button before he heard the latch click and then Evelyn was surveying him through the half-open doorway and revealing just enough of herself to show him pink stretch pants and a shaggy, loose-fitting white sweater.

"Oh," she said flatly. "You again."

Standish, hat in hand, did what he could with a smile. He had not expected a welcome or any real cooperation but he thought he had an opening wedge that would at least get him inside.

When she said: "Is this a continuation of yesterday's session?" he said: "I've just talked to Mrs. Choate. You know, I wasn't able to reach her yesterday, and she mentioned a couple of points I thought you might be able to clarify."

The statement was apparently ambiguous enough to whet her curiosity because the door opened wide and she said, with some reluctance and no enthusiasm: "Very well. Come in."

She turned to let him follow her and close the door. This

gave him a full view of the stretch pants, which were snug
as a pair of tights, revealing beautifully shaped legs and a
compact bottom that moved with confidence and grace.

On the left of the hall was a dining room with a mahogany
table and silver gleaming from the sideboard. There was an
old linen chest across the hall with an oil painting of someone's ancestor above it. Just beyond was the entrance to the
living room. Here there was no wall-to-wall carpeting but
wide-board floors and Oriental rugs and a sizable fireplace
and, at the rear beyond the double doors, a porch and ter-
race.

"This is most attractive," Standish said, genuinely impressed and forgetting the woman for a moment. Apparently
she noted the sincerity of his tone and the black eyes considered him again.

"The room?"

"The whole thing. The house is old, isn't it? I mean, you
didn't build it to look old?"

"Oh, it's old enough. Robert's grandfather built it." She
waved him toward a chair and perched on the edge of the
sofa opposite the fireplace, clasped hands propped on one
knee. "What was it you wanted to say?"

Standish adjusted himself to the transition from one
woman to the other. Where, at Marion Choate's place, there
had been warmth and good humor, here there was more
beauty and an air of coolness, reserve, and formality. There
would, he knew, be no offer of a drink and he was afraid
that any information he might get would have to be forced.
He considered again her dark beauty, the shining black hair,
the straight patrician nose, the flawless complexion.

"Mrs. Choate and I were talking about the accident."

"So I gathered."

"We agreed that except for your husband it tended to
solve some problems."

"Problems?"

"According to her, her marriage had been on the rocks for

some time. She expects to get a more generous settlement than she would have, say, six months ago. She hinted," he added, stretching the truth a little, "that you might marry Warren Choate after the divorce is final. . . . You can decline to answer on any grounds you choose, but is that so?"

For an instant he thought he saw a flicker of humor in the dark eyes before she said: "It's a possibility, yes."

"Because of the accident would you say that Donald Tremaine is more desirable marriage material than he was?"

"If you mean in a material way, yes."

"He never married?"

"No."

"No regular girl friends?"

"You mean as of now?"

"Yes."

"I wouldn't want to say."

"How about in the past?"

"In the past there were one or two he may have been seriously interested in. Unfortunately at the time his salary was around eight thousand or eighty-five hundred and that just wasn't enough to consider seriously. Not for the girls I have in mind. He never was what you'd call a ladies' man. He seemed shy and fumbling and uncertain. Or maybe he just lacked self-confidence in that particular area."

"Did he inherit anything from your husband's personal estate—I don't mean the insurance?"

"He didn't need anything."

"Oh?"

"There was a trust fund set up by his father."

Standish had not heard of this before and his dark-blue eyes grew attentive and thoughtful as he sought some way to amplify the statement.

"A trust fund still in existence at his age?" he said. "Why was that?"

"I suppose it was the way the father felt about Donald. I didn't know him then but from what I understand he was a moody, difficult child and the more his father tried to re-make him in his image, the more Donald rebelled. He had some trouble in two prep schools. I guess he was what you'd call a loner."

She settled herself more comfortably and said, not look-ing at him now: "As I understand it, he didn't want any-thing to do with team activities and whatever disciplinary action had to be taken seemed to make him just that much more stubborn. He barely squeaked through college. He was drafted and served two years in the army but I don't know anything about that phase of his life. I do know that when he came back he would have nothing to do with the family business. So when Mr. Tremaine drew up his will he took all that into consideration. Robert was six years older and Robert had conformed. He did well both in prep school and in college and earned letters in football in both schools. He seemed to like the family business and his father had confidence in him. He even approved of me, the father I mean.

"He was not a wealthy man but he was reasonably well off and the business was doing all right. He had too much conscience to cut Donald off completely, so he made Robert executor and trustee. When he died and the estate was set-tled Robert took his half and acted as trustee for Donald's share until Donald's thirty-fifth birthday."

"When will that be?" Standish asked.

"In about two years, I think. Robert was pretty conserva-tive with the investments he made but I think Donald's share has increased a few thousand even so. Something over a hundred thousand all told."

"And upon your husband's death, the trust was termi-nated and the funds paid to Donald?"

She did not answer this but she was looking at him now, eyes narrowing and her lips compressed.

"I suppose this bolsters your conviction that the accident was a good thing for all of us except Robert."

Standish ducked that one and said: "When I talked to you yesterday afternoon the police were looking for Ralph Estey. A few hours later they found him."

"I know. I saw the morning paper. It says he committed suicide."

"I don't think it said that in so many words. Newspapers have to be careful. I think what you read said that *according to the police* the fatal wound *may* have been self-inflicted."

"And you disagree?"

"For now, yes."

"Why?"

"For several reasons. One is that I knew Estey pretty well."

Her smile was fixed now, the dark gaze hostile. "What was your medical specialty, Doctor?"

"Why—internal medicine."

"Then you had no advanced training in psychology or psychiatry or the reading of men's minds? And yet on the basis of some acquaintanceship with a man you can state categorically that he did not commit suicide?"

"If Ralph Estey committed suicide," Standish said evenly, "there could only be one reason, under the circumstances."

"And that is?"

"That he murdered Jess Flemming the night before. If he murdered Flemming then I'll admit he could have committed suicide."

"I thought the official view was that he did murder Flemming."

"It is the official view."

"And you think you can change it?"

"Until I'm convinced that they're right I have to try."

"Nonsense." Her voice was clipped, irritable. "That Flemming man and Ralph Estey had a fight on the sidewalk outside Hennessey's Friday night."

"How do you know?"

The red mouth opened instantly and she closed it. It was

the first time Standish had ever seen her disconcerted. "Well—Donald happened to see part of it."

"And you and Warren Choate had been there all evening and Donald came in and told you."

"Well—yes. He said Estey had said something about a gun and made a threat. What possible reason is there for believing that he didn't walk in on Flemming Monday night and carry out the threat?"

"A little pinch of chloral hydrate."

"A pinch of what?" she said, a deep frown marring the smoothness of her complexion.

Standish told her about chloral hydrate and what it could do. He added a few explanatory words to his hypothesis.

"If the police are right," he added, "then there's no way it can ever be proved that Ralph Estey did not commit suicide. But until I get some reasonable explanation for the presence of chloral hydrate in Jess Flemming's body—"

"But why should you care?" she said, her voice harsh.

"Because"—Standish took a second to be sure of his answer—"I don't like to see anyone get away with murder. Someone gave Flemming that drug and I say it wasn't Estey. Then who did? Why?"

Expecting no answer, he said: "So far I've only been able to come up with one possibility I can accept. Which could very well go back to the accident that killed your husband last December. Vehicular homicide is hard to prove. I'm not sure I can. I'm not sure of anything—yet. But when you get your thoughts in the right channel it's not too difficult to understand how that accident could have been planned."

She came to her feet in one abrupt, jerky motion, fists at her sides and the dark eyes curious and, perhaps, a little scared.

"I don't have to listen to this."

"No, you don't. But since I'm almost through, why not give me another minute? If someone did deliberately kill your husband, wouldn't you like to know about it?"

"Flemming killed him."

"Exactly. But with his record—you can look it up—you can understand that he's the type who could be hired for the job. Your husband's drinking habits were no secret," he went on quickly before she could interrupt. "He was a Saturday-night drunk and very often at Hennessey's. Was it coincidence that a man like Flemming was conveniently parked down the street just far enough to fake such an accident? Or was he waiting there deliberately, having been tipped off that you and your husband were always the last to leave. He was sitting in his car at the right time, having a little trouble getting it started, so he said. It wouldn't take much of a signal to alert him. As a matter of fact he wouldn't even need a signal. All he had to do was keep his eyes open. Your husband comes staggering out into the middle of the street. You saw the car, the headlights."

"Of course I saw them."

"Sometimes," Standish said, his voice more considerate, "a long time after a thing like that has happened, a person will remember a detail or an impression that escaped him earlier. Is there anything more you can tell me about it?"

He watched her shake her head, saw her gaze drop. After a moment she took a deep breath.

"No," she said, her anger gone. "Frankly, I've been trying my best to forget it."

"At the hearing it seemed like a miracle that you escaped uninjured. As I recall it," he added, "you fell, but the car did not actually touch you."

"I still don't know why," she said. "I think it was Robert. I think that somehow, drunk as he was, he must have realized what was happening. He could have pushed me just enough to get me out of the way but I could never be sure. All I'll ever remember is the lights of that car and the sound of the motor and the scream of the brakes and that awful crash."

Standish nodded and let his breath ease out. There was,

he knew, nothing more that could be added now. In his own mind nothing changed. Having brought up again the subject of the accident he could not bully this woman in her present distressed condition. He had added a little to his growing fund of information and now, as politely and considerately as he could, he thanked her for her time and apologized for bothering her. She was still watching him, not moving or giving any sign that she had heard, as he backed into the hall and started for the front door.

13

MARY HAYWARD had changed to a street dress and seemed about to leave when Paul Standish returned to his office. He still wanted to see Donald Tremaine and possibly Warren Choate, but he did not think they would be home from the office at this hour so he decided to wait until later before he tried to see them.

"Only two calls, Doctor," Mary said, and mentioned the names of the patients and the nature of the ailments. "They wanted to see you this afternoon but both decided they could wait. I told them that you would stop in as soon as you could in the morning."

Standish, glancing in his appointment book, nodded. "Good enough." He sat down, aware now of a certain weariness as he let his body relax. He wondered if he should suggest dinner. Before he could make up his mind the telephone rang and Mary reached for it.

"Dr. Standish's office. Yes. . . . Who? Well—just a minute, please," she added doubtfully, and looked at Standish. "It's Lou Cheney."

Standish held out his hand and she surrendered the instrument. "Yes, Lou."

"I'm in the neighborhood. I thought I'd stop by. Okay?"

"Sure."

"Five minutes."

Mary accepted the telephone, cradled it, her gray eyes mirroring her surprise before the disapproval began to show.

"Lou Cheney," she said, knowing the nature of the man's work and accepting him no more than she did Lieutenant Ballard. "What does he want?"

"He's been checking out a couple of things for me."

"Since when?"

"Since last evening."

"Officially?" she said, persisting. "I mean for the city? Or will you have to pay him out of your own pocket?"

"It's hard to tell at this point. Don't you think my personal budget will stand it?"

"Oh, I'm sure it will. It's just that I don't understand you." She paused, no longer smiling and some inner disturbance apparent in her inflection. "I don't mean that literally," she said, trying again. "It's just that ever since Monday you seemed more interested in being a medical examiner—or even some kind of detective—than you have in being a doctor."

"I made my house calls this morning, didn't I?" Standish said patiently.

"Yes."

"I saw everyone who had an appointment during office hours. You've already said that the two calls that came later can just as well be taken care of in the morning."

She seemed about to reply and then something happened to make her change her mind.

"Whatever you say, Doctor." Her small smile was professional and polite. "Will that be all for now?"

"You're sure you don't want to stay and listen in to what Cheney has to say?"

"Quite sure."

"We might even work in the dinner we missed last night," Standish said, not really caring at the moment but feeling that he should make the offer.

"No thank you." She made a point of glancing at her wristwatch. "I have other plans this evening."

She was gone then and a minute or so later Lou Cheney came in shaking his head.

"I just passed that good-looking nurse of yours down on the sidewalk," he complained. "I gave her one of my best 'Good afternoon, Miss Haywards,' and all I got was a frosty nod. I don't think she likes me."

Standish grinned and said it was nothing personal. He said it was just Mary's reaction to her disapproval of other things, specifically his medical-examiner duties. He watched Cheney get rid of his hat and coat and slouch in the patient's chair opposite the desk while he reached for a cigarette.

He was, Standish realized, a very average-looking individual—in height, weight, build, and appearance. He wore a brown suit, brown oxfords, a white shirt, a plain-colored tie. In almost any gathering Cheney would be unnoticeable. Passing in the street he would seldom rate more than a glance, which was part of his stock in trade and added greatly to his effectiveness. He had eight years of big-city police training and five with a national agency before striking out on his own. He was the part-time representative of the same agency but he had his own office and at forty-five he was married, owned his own home, had three children, and rarely carried a gun. Now, having lighted his cigarette and inhaled, he produced a small notebook and opened it on the desk.

"What do you want first?"

"Suit yourself," Standish said.

"The social business with Warren Choate was not too difficult. Like I told you over the phone yesterday afternoon,

5

sometimes one job rubs against another in this business. We'd already done some research. I can't tell you why or for whom but Choate has been having dinner once a week or so with a real good-looking brunette."

"Who?"

"I can't be sure because I haven't been on this other job too long. In fact I haven't been handling it personally. The woman always wears dark glasses and usually a scarf on her hair, but it's black. Very simply dressed, inconspicuous, quiet. They eat in obscure places. They go for drives." He glanced up. "Any of this help?"

"It's a start. What about Mrs. Choate?"

"All I can tell you there is that she sees no one in particular in town. She goes to New York once a week—we haven't had time to check her out at that end—sometimes for the day. Sometimes she stays overnight. Sometimes she drives; other times she parks her car at the station and takes the train."

"That fits," Standish said. "She told me this afternoon that she has a man in the city. She said she'd probably marry him when she gets the divorce. . . . Anything on Evelyn Tremaine?"

"Nothing specific. I haven't had enough time to get much there but we did have a little luck with the brother— Donald."

Standish nodded and Cheney said: "You know the place he lives?"

Standish said no, and Cheney, consulting his notebook, mentioned an address. "One of those narrow-front brick houses that have been remodeled. Four apartments, one to the floor. The owner has the ground-floor apartment and he's not only nosy, he has some trouble with insomnia. For a ten-dollar bill he's not against a little gossip."

"You talked to him?"

"One of my men did." Cheney leaned back, looking a little pleased with himself. "It seems," he said, "that Donald

has a lady friend who calls on him once a week on the average. After dark. Usually around nine or ten. The landlord
figures she must leave plenty late, because he never sees
her go."

Standish waited while a spark of excitement began to
glow inside him. "A brunette, by any chance?"

"Yep."

"Any other description?"

"Not much. The place is in the middle of the block and
there isn't much light. Every time he's seen her she's been
wearing dark glasses. He seems to think she has a nice figure
but since she's always wearing a coat he can't be sure."

"Does he remember the last time she was there?"

"Sunday." Cheney crossed his legs and made a comment
not in his notes. "It sort of looks," he said, "like our brunette
with the dark glasses could be giving both boys a play,
hunh?"

Standish nodded absently. It took a while to digest what
he had heard and to finish with his speculation. Only then
was he ready for further information.

"What about the banks?"

"There too," Cheney said, "I got a break. I started at the
City National on Elm Street because Choate has his offices
in the building. Luckily, all four of them have accounts
there. I've done some work for the City National in the past
and I know an assistant cashier pretty well. He was willing
to talk a little, off the record and without being too specific,
so long as I tell him it's confidential and a personal favor."

He consulted his notes and said: "With Choate we're nowhere. His account is too healthy and too active to show
anything special around the date you're interested in."

"You mean in December?"

"Yeah. Mrs. Choate has had an account there for some
years, never very large. Recently she's been making a
monthly deposit of her separation payments. The cashier
won't say how much."

He glanced again at his notebook. "About the same thing with Mrs. Tremaine. Had a modest account for years. A three-figure—those are the cashier's words not mine—average monthly balance. Until about a month after the accident. Some insurance payment, according to the cashier, brought it up to six figures."

Standish said he knew about the insurance payment. "There wasn't any sizable deposit or withdrawal before that? . . . Okay," he added when Cheney shook his head. "How about Donald Tremaine?"

"Until after the accident he kept just about enough in his account to keep from paying the monthly service charge. Then the insurance company kicks in. About the same amount as the woman got."

"How about now?"

"For who?"

"Well—Mrs. Tremaine."

"She still has a healthy balance but she's been investing it in stocks and bonds over the past couple of months, probably through Warren Choate's brokerage office. The same with Donald. I'm only guessing about where he's investing his money but I'd assume he'd do it through the family firm. He also had one big withdrawal."

"For a hundred thousand," Standish said, remembering that Tremaine had bought himself a partnership in the firm of Certified Public Accountants he had been working for on salary.

"I don't know about the amount," Cheney said, "but the cashier did mention some big payment to a firm of C.P.A.'s."

"But nothing around the time of the accident? Say a week before or a week after?"

"Nothing that I could get." Cheney started to close his notebook and Standish thought of something else.

"What about Jess Flemming? Did you get any line on him?"

"Hahh!" Cheney grunted softly. "Hoods like Flemming

don't have bank accounts. Maybe a safe-deposit box if they have any loot. Most of them, all they've got is front and what dough they have is in their pants pocket. But I did ask around about him. I got a little here, a little there."

He pocketed his notebook and said: "Flemming was never big-time. You wanted a muscle job done he'd do it. The word is that in the past he's taken a contract or two to put a guy away. Well, a couple of weeks after the hearing he blows town. One of my contacts said he thought Flemming went to Las Vegas so I telephoned a guy I know that has a little business there. He called me back. From what he could get Flemming had been on the West Coast and stopped in Vegas on the way East. He wasn't working. At least not at any job my friend knew about. He stayed at a motel and took it easy. Played around with a broad or two from time to time, showed up for a little play at the tables some nights. He turned up here a couple of weeks ago with a big car. A Lincoln. Not new but not one you could pick up for twelve or fifteen hundred bucks either. Since then he's just been around." He stood up. "I guess that's about it, Doc."

Standish came to his feet, his angular face grave and the dark-blue eyes thoughtful under the straight brows. Keeping his thoughts on the financial information he now had, he realized that only in Flemming had he any support for his theory. Flemming had obviously come into some money, and at the proper time. He could have been hired to run down Robert Tremaine. But by whom? . . .

"What?" he said, aware that Cheney had spoken.

"I just asked you if that would wrap it up for you?"

"It helps," he said, "and thanks. I'd like to keep you working a little longer. Could you, or one of your men, keep an eye on Donald Tremaine?"

"Well"—Cheney shrugged and looked doubtful—"I suppose so. That's what we're in business for. What do you have in mind?"

"I'm going around to Tremaine's place after dinner and have a talk with him," Standish said. "I'd like to have somebody watch the place after I leave."

"In case our mysterious brunette shows up again?"

"Something like that. From what I've been able to get he's never had a reputation as a ladies' man. I'm curious to know whether someone came along to change his attitude."

"You'll be seeing him around maybe eight-thirty or nine?"

"Probably. If he's in."

"Okay." Cheney slipped on his coat and reached for his hat. "Around nine or so I'll have someone there. Suppose the brunette shows?"

"Just stay with it."

"Until she comes out?"

"Right."

"And after that," Cheney said, grinning now as he backed toward the door, "you want us to tail her and find out who she is."

"If you can."

"Will do. Do you want me to call you in the morning or will you get in touch with me?"

Standish, a little uncertain of his plans and quite possibly influenced by his thoughts of Mary Hayward, said he would call Cheney.

14

IT WAS after nine when Paul Standish parked his car in the quiet tree-lined street where Donald Tremaine lived. The address he sought was, as Lou Cheney had described it, in the middle of the block, a narrow-front stone-and-brick building that looked as if it had been there at least fifty years. Light glowed behind curtains of the front windows on all four floors and the wood-and-glass door giving on the vestibule was unlocked. There were four mailboxes recessed in the right-hand wall and enough illumination came through the frosted-glass panel of the second door to tell him that Tremaine occupied the second floor.

There was a pushbutton and a voice tube over each mailbox but as Standish glanced round he saw that the edge of the inner door had been warped or swollen by the weather and no longer fitted properly. This made the lock inoperative and a push got him inside without difficulty. A single round fixture dangled from a high ceiling to light the squarish foyer with a front-to-back hallway and stairs mounting straight ahead on the left.

Donald Tremaine had a highball glass in his hand when he opened the door and his bespectacled glance showed momentary surprise as recognition came to him. He smiled politely and there was nothing reluctant about the gesture he made by opening the door wider and stepping back.

"Well, hello, Doctor. Come in."

"Your front door was ajar," Standish said. "So I didn't bother to ring."

"Perfectly all right. It's been that way for over a month. Warped, I guess. The landlord is always going to fix it but never does. . . . Toss your coat anywhere. Let me fix you a drink."

Standish put his hat aside but he kept his coat on, saying he wouldn't be long. He said he thought he'd skip the drink. "It hasn't been too long since I finished dinner."

"Same with me," Tremaine said. "But I seem to have developed a habit of having a brandy and soda afterward when I'm home. Seems to settle my stomach and help the digestive processes."

He waved a hand in a gesture that took in all of the room. "Sit down."

It was a nice room, Standish decided. Different, colorful, not exactly masculine but not feminine either. The carpet was pastel gray, the antique maple pieces—the kneehole desk, the highboy, the occasional tables—were well cared for. Birch logs stood on brass andirons in the blackened fireplace; there were two overstuffed wing chairs done in some maroon material, and the divan with its matching pillows was covered in an off-white, rough-textured fabric that looked expensive. Standish sat down here and was faced again with the problem of what to say or where to start. To get a little time he reached for a cigarette. Tremaine stepped forward and snapped flame from a lighter on the coffee table.

"Thanks," Standish said. "I talked to Mrs. Choate and your sister-in-law this afternoon."

"Oh?" Tremaine's brows climbed above the metal-rimmed spectacles. "About what?"

"Several things, including you."

"Me?" The brows stayed high. "For heaven's sake why?"

Standish ducked the direct question. "I hadn't known about the trust fund your father left. Didn't it bother you to have your brother in control until you were thirty-five?"

"Certainly it bothered me."

"He could have handed over your half before that, couldn't he?"

"Of course he could."

Tremaine, standing in front of the fireplace, propped one elbow on the mantelpiece. He was wearing slacks, a white woolen shirt, open at the throat and topped by a knotted foulard scarf. His brown hair was carefully combed. Small-boned but well proportioned, he had about him an air that was immaculate and fastidious, and Standish had the impression that this was a man who would make it a point to look proper and well groomed under any and all circumstances.

"But he didn't."

"If you knew Robert you'd know why. He was his father's son. He measured up and toed the line. He was a lot older than I was and he set an example I didn't care to follow."

Standish nodded, dark gaze speculative as he waited out the pause that followed. He remembered what the two women had said, not the exact words but reasonable synonyms. Shy. Moody, naïve, a loner. A boy who never quite conformed.

"I was the only one who gave my father any trouble," Tremaine went on, distance in his voice now. "Somehow I was a reflection on the rugged, he-man tradition that had been established. . . . I suppose it was my refusal to start in as an office boy in the family business that really tore it. I'd taken some accounting courses in college. I like figures and I was fairly good at math. So I took some more courses on my own and got my own job. That's when father made the will."

"You and your brother didn't get along?" Standish said, wanting to keep the other talking.

"We had very little in common if that's what you mean. Robert was aggressive in his living, in business, with women and, later, with his drinking. He liked the hold he had on me, the feeling of power if you like. He could be pretty damn patronizing when he wanted to be and with me at least he got to be rather hard to take."

There had been a rising and resentful inflection in his tone as he spoke, and, as though finally aware of this, Tremaine digressed.

"Look. You're sure you won't change your mind about a drink?" He held up his own glass to show that it was empty. "I'm afraid I need a refill. Will you excuse me?"

He disappeared down the hallway and Standish stood up and moved to the mantelpiece. A large silver-framed photograph stood at each end. One showed a pleasant-faced, graying woman that he assumed to be Tremaine's mother;

the other was a photograph of a handsome, robust-looking man flanked by the two Tremaine boys. Taken some years ago, it showed the difference in the two brothers, and it was when Standish moved it slightly to cut down the reflection of light on the glass that he saw the gold-and-enamel object which had been left behind the frame.

It looked like a small cigarette lighter until he lifted the arm on top and pressed it. The misty spray that the plunger expelled had a strong, spicy smell which fell on the front of his coat and he realized too late that he had activated a perfume atomizer.

He put it back, the strong scent still in the back of his throat. He moved to the divan again, a faint frown working around his eyes now and his mind busy. It may have been the knowledge that a woman had been here that made him more alert. More probably it was the off-white background of the fabric and some trick of light that enabled him to see a glistening strand of hair that had been caught by the rough fabric of one pillow.

He could see, as he looked closer, that the hair was black and as he lifted it carefully between thumb and forefinger he knew it was about a foot long. Thinking hard now and brows warped, he acted not on any specific conclusion but simply as a matter of habit. Taking his notebook from his coat pocket, he opened it to two clean facing pages. He lowered the hair carefully. It curled somewhat of its own accord and against the whiteness of the paper he was reassured that the strand was black.

He said, unconsciously and half aloud: "Hmmm," and as his mind went on it seemed now that he had conclusive proof that Donald Tremaine was not quite the character the two women had pictured that afternoon. To believe them now was to assume that they were mistaken in their conviction that Tremaine was naïve and ingenuous with women and had no luck with them.

Lou Cheney's talk with the landlord and the weekly woman visitor had dispelled the original impression and here was additional corroboration. Already his mind had come up with a rough idea of what he might do with the hair, but before he could dwell on the subject Tremaine came back with his refill. It was instantly apparent from his manner that something had happened in the kitchen and he proceeded to explain what it was.

"I got to thinking out in the kitchen," he said, not impolitely but with a cool and studied skepticism. "You didn't come here to talk about my father's will or that trust fund. Did you?"

"Well—no."

"You're a very easy man to talk to, Doctor. Or maybe it's just that I'm one of those trusting souls who like to be pleasant to everyone. It's about that man Flemming and the suicide of the trumpet player, isn't it?"

"Estey hadn't been found when I talked to you yesterday afternoon," Standish said. "But I guess you know what happened to him?"

"The police seem to think he shot himself. Don't you agree?"

"No."

"Why?"

Standish thought it over and, seeing no easy out, decided to be frank.

"That's a hard question to answer. I could say that in my opinion, both as a man and as a physician, I don't think Estey would kill himself that way. I knew him fairly well. I thought I understood what made him tick, but that's only a personal opinion and to give it any validity I'd have to go back a little and say I don't think Estey shot Flemming Monday night. I could be more specific in a medical way but I don't know why you should be interested in the details. Let's just say that as a medical examiner I discovered certain irregularities that seem suspicious."

He hesitated, choosing his words with care. "You can call it a theory if you like. Call it idle speculation if you want to, but either way the idea is based on the remote possibility that Flemming's murder was no coincidence and did not come as a result of a quarrel between him and Estey but instead was planned that way."

"Planned?" Some new tension showed in Tremaine's good-looking face. Behind the glasses his eyes were narrowed and intent. "By whom?"

"I don't know."

"For what reason?"

"To answer that," Standish said, "I have to go back to your brother's accident. On the face of it that's all it was—an accident, pure and simple. I had no reason to doubt it until now. But vehicular homicide is a tricky thing," he added. "I could give you chapter and verse and show you pieces written by more experienced and more learned men than me. My point is this:

"Because of the circumstances and your brother's condition, because of the testimony of his wife and the doorman at Hennessey's, because of my tests for the percentage of blood alcohol both in Flemming and in your brother, he was let off lightly. On the other hand, Flemming, from what I've learned about him, is the sort who could be hired for such a job if someone was clever enough to recognize the possibilities of a traffic murder."

He put up a hand and spoke quickly to forestall an impending interruption. "For the sake of argument, let's say someone *did* hire Flemming and pay him off. Suppose Flemming spent the money and then realized what a wonderful extortion setup he had. Under such circumstances the one who hired him might decide that the only way he could ever be free from the threat, the only way to avoid a possible lifetime of payments, was to murder the man who threatened him."

He stood up, aware that Tremaine was watching him.

"Before you throw the theory away let me get the rest of it off my chest."

Tremaine remembered his drink and took a big swallow. He put the glass down on the mantelpiece and then, folding his arms, leaned against the edge of it.

"Go ahead," he said, his voice quietly contemptuous. "You're my guest. You have the floor."

His sarcasm was wasted on Standish because he was thinking hard and wanted to get his thoughts in order.

"To make it stand up—I mean the conclusion that Estey shot Flemming and then killed himself—the idea would have to be predicated on the known fact that Flemming and Estey had tangled over a girl named Sheila Keith, that Estey had been knocked out and had made the threat that he had a gun and intended to use it the next time Flemming got in his way." He hesitated just a second and said: "You were a witness to that fight, weren't you?"

The question seemed to take Tremaine aback. The eyes blinked and were no longer so intent. It took him two or three seconds to frame an answer and it sounded more hesitant than emphatic.

"Well—yes. I mean, when I got there Estey was on his back and you were tending to him. I didn't know what happened or what went on before that."

"But you were there in time to hear the threat."

"All right, I heard what Estey said. What about it?"

"When you went inside you joined your sister-in-law and Warren Choate. You told them what you saw."

He reached for his hat and got a whiff of his perfumed lapel. When Tremaine made no comment, he moved to the door.

"What I'm saying, and it's not an accusation or, at the moment, even an inference, is that at least three people and possibly four benefited greatly by your brother's death. Three of you had sufficient knowledge to plan a murder and suicide the police would accept."

He waited before he turned the doorknob. Tremaine seemed not to have moved a muscle. He was still leaning back against the mantelpiece, arms folded across his chest. From that distance Standish could not tell what was going on behind the thin-rimmed glasses and when there was still no reply he opened the door and went out.

Downstairs the main door was still stuck and unlatched. As he came out on the sidewalk and turned toward his car he remembered Lou Cheney and the assignment that had been given to him. There was no one else on the sidewalk, no shadows that moved. He counted ten parked cars in the block, all of them looking dark and empty. As he climbed into his own sedan he wondered again if Cheney or one of his men was watching the house, and whether the time would be wasted.

15

PAUL STANDISH spent three quarters of an hour trying to locate Warren Choate and then decided he could wait until morning. He did not expect the broker would offer any information but he hoped to find out if any of the people he was interested in had made a stock sale through the Choate office around the time of the accident.

By the time he had given up on Choate, he wanted the drink he had refused from Donald Tremaine, and he went once more to Hennessey's. Business was reasonably good and the band was in action. Hennessey had found a new trumpet man, a plump youth who hit the right notes and improvised well, but to Standish the group lacked the driving precision Ralph Estey had always been able to produce.

It had been his original intention to have this drink at the bar but the sight of Sheila Keith, who was working with a plump and tinted redhead as her assistant, changed his mind. Even when he asked if she could sit with him and have a drink he did not realize the motivation behind his request. He was pleased when she said yes and led the way to this obscure table in the rear corner, but it was not until the drink came that he understood that what he really wanted was someone to talk to.

He could not go to Ballard because he had nothing new to add to his earlier statement regarding his skepticism about the police theory. The talks he had had, the suspicion that to him seemed increasingly valid, meant nothing. It might not even sound convincing to his own ears when spoken aloud. Had it been earlier he might have called Mary Hayward, who had become his sounding board and sympathetic listener. Now, with Sheila Keith watching him and waiting for some clue as to what he had in mind, it suddenly seemed important that he make a case for himself and get her reaction.

She was wearing her customary simple dark dress with a white collar, which was her Hennessey uniform. She had more makeup on than usual and he could understand why. The practiced smile which was her trademark was missing now that she was at ease, and the upward-slanting green eyes, shadowed and expertly lined, remained watchful and attentive.

"I've been asking a lot of questions today," he said. "I still think you're right about Ralph."

"I am? You mean about not killing himself?"

Standish nodded.

"Then he didn't kill Jess Flemming either."

"Right."

"But the police—"

"I know what *they* think."

"And you think they're wrong? Why? Do you know something they don't?"

Standish sorted out the questions and tried to remember what he had said. It wasn't easy. There had been no specific routine in his interviews with Marion Choate and Evelyn and Donald Tremaine. He had been fishing for information and his questions and statements were impromptu. He recalled that he had mentioned the chloral hydrate to Mary. He was not sure about the others but he did not think Sheila knew the basis for his original suspicion. He decided to find out.

"Do you know what chloral hydrate is?"

"I think so. Some kind of drug, isn't it? If you put it in someone's drink it knocks you out pretty quick?"

"That's about right. It used to be standard equipment in some off-limits bars and nightclubs. It made an easy way for a hooker or a waiter or someone to roll a visiting fireman before they tossed him out on the street."

"Yes." She was nodding her agreement and her small painted mouth fashioned a smile. "I've worked in places where they used something like that once in a while." She paused to let the statement sink in, the smile still there, before she added: "But not just that way."

"Oh?"

"These weren't the kind of traps you're talking about. They were respectable enough. But sometimes some prominent citizen or local bigshot would come in. He might even be a regular out on the town. He'd keep putting away drinks and then later he might get loud and boisterous and objectionable. The management wouldn't want to throw him out so the bartender would slip a little something in his drink and before you knew it he'd be quiet enough. Probably asleep at his table and it was easy to get him out and put him in a taxi and see that he got home. Would that be

what your chloral hydrate does? Why? What does that have
to do with Ralph?"

Standish took some of his drink and leaned forward, his
manner confidential. He told her about the "powder paper"
he had found and just how he had happened to see it. He
said that the few grains that had remained stuck to the paper had been analyzed by the city chemist and that the
toxicologist who made further tests was ready to state that
Jess Flemming had ingested some chloral hydrate not too
long before he died.

He had her full attention by the time he finished. The
green eyes were wide open and the mouth slack, the drink
in front of her forgotten. It took her a few seconds to realize
he had finished and then she said:

"And you told the police this? What did they say?"

"Oh, they had some answers. I'm not sure Lieutenant
Ballard believes them but until he gets some proof that he's
wrong he has to stick with them. He says that Estey could
have called on Flemming, offered to call off the feud, and
conned him into taking a drink that he had fixed."

She shook her head. "Never."

"He even suggested," Standish said, "that someone could
have come in earlier—maybe you—and had a drink or two
with Flemming. Somewhere along the line he was drugged
and set up so Ralph could come in a little later and use the
gun."

"Oh, for God's sake!" Her mouth dipped at the corners
and her voice was contemptuous. "That lieutenant must be
out of his mind." She paused again, still angry with the in-
sinuation. When Standish made no immediate reply she
said: "How do *you* think Flemming got the chloral hydrate?"

"Oh, I think he took it in a drink all right. I think that fight
out on the sidewalk Friday night was the lucky break that
made it easier. The police were bound to find out about it.
With Flemming shot to death they have to go looking for

Estey. When they find him an apparent suicide the case is
wrapped up."

"But who? Why?"

"I don't know who, but I've got an idea why."

Standish went on quickly then, speaking frankly and
easily as he unburdened himself of the things that had been
piling up in his mind. He spoke again of the accident and
the ramifications of vehicular homicide long used by gang-
sters as a method of murder. He said that Flemming's previous record and background in violence suggested that he
would be familiar with such methods and, if the price was
right and the planning sound, he was the type who could
do the job.

"Oh, he could," she said. "He could."

Standish went on as though he had not heard. He said
that Flemming had become more affluent since the accident. He mentioned the trip to the West Coast and Las
Vegas, the big car which was a more recent purchase.

"Suppose Flemming was running out of cash and realized
he had a perfect way to get more, maybe indefinitely?" He
did not wait for a reply but repeated the hypothesis he had
given Donald Tremaine earlier, sketching the ingredients
needed to work out a practical murder-suicide case. "Everyone benefited by Robert Tremaine's death," he said, and
outlined the financial benefits that had accrued to the
Choates and to Evelyn and Donald Tremaine.

She was looking right at him now, leaning closer, so that
he could see only the intriguing depth of her green eyes.

"Yes," she breathed. "They all gained something, didn't
they? But which one hired Flemming? I mean, if you're
right how can you—"

Standish interrupted, knowing what she was about to say.
"I don't know." He leaned back to finish his drink. "I want
to talk to Warren Choate. I couldn't find him tonight. Maybe
in the morning I can find out if someone sold, say, five or

ten thousand dollars' worth of stock about the time of the accident."

"You mean, to get the cash to pay Flemming?"

Standish nodded. "I also know that Donald Tremaine may not be quite the proper, innocent-looking bachelor he seems." He passed along the information he had received from Marion Choate and Evelyn Tremaine that afternoon and shook his head. "I'm not so sure they're right about Donald," he said. "I know that he has been entertaining some woman on the average of one night a week for some time now. No one knows who she is—yet. But I'm pretty sure I can find out before long. He used to be an eighty-five-hundred-a-year bookkeeper. Now he's a partner in a good business with maybe a couple of hundred thousand more to back him up."

"Yes," she said, "I see what you mean." And then, out of nowhere, she added: "You don't give up easily, do you, Doctor?"

Standish found the question as surprising as it was direct. He had not thought of himself that way and he did not know how to answer. As he considered this she posed another question.

"Are you doing all this just because you were a friend of Ralph's?"

"Maybe," he said, and the more he thought about it, the less sure he was of himself. He couldn't say that as a doctor and a medical examiner he could not accept the unexplained presence of chloral hydrate in a man who had been shot in the chest. He could not say that to him it was important that the proper answers be listed in any report he made. "The lieutenant and I talked to Ralph's ex-wife last night," he said. "I guess you know he had a five-year-old son."

"Yes, I did."

"Ralph was paying twenty-five a week for the boy's support. There was also a ten-thousand-dollar insurance policy on his life. It had a suicide clause in it. If the verdict stands as suicide there will be no payment for the boy's education. Maybe it's just that—well, if Ralph did *not* commit suicide I'd like to have a hand in getting at the truth."

As he finished, his mind slid off on a tangent and he thought again about the gold-and-enamel perfume atomizer, the spray of which he could still smell. He remembered the black hair that was now in his notebook He knew what he was going to do with it. With luck he could find another for comparison purposes. He did not speak of this now because he suddenly realized that he had been using this girl as a sounding board without regard for her personal feelings or welfare.

"I'm sorry, Sheila," he said. "I didn't mean to bend your ear this way."

"Oh, that's all right. I just hope you *can* finally prove the truth about Ralph."

"And what are your plans?"

She took a deep breath and looked down at the table. "I don't know. This morning I thought I'd just quit and get away from here. I've been breaking Madge in"—she tipped her head backward toward the checkroom—"and she'd like the job. But then—I don't know. This is the best spot—for money, I mean—I've had in a long time. Maybe I'll just go away for a week or two if it's all right with Mr. Hennessey."

Standish nodded. He said it might be a good idea. For another second or two he eyed her with approval, impressed not only by her attractiveness but by her courage and determination. Then, all at once, he was embarrassed because he knew he had no right to look at her like that. He signaled the waiter and paid the check. He was still a little embarrassed when she helped him on with his coat and he said good-night.

It had been cloudy early in the evening, and by ignoring the threat of rain Paul Standish found himself caught without a raincoat as he stepped out on a sidewalk that was

slick and black and wet. The doorman, hovering in the
shadows, snapped open his oversized umbrella. He offered
to walk Standish across the street to the parking lot but
Standish said it wasn't raining that hard and, making sure
that no car was coming, he loped over to the parking lot
and piled into his car. He found the seat wet from an open
window and rolled it up. He dug his keys out of his pocket,
got the motor going, and activated the windshield wiper. He
lit a cigarette from the dashboard lighter and when he still
could not locate the attendant he jockeyed his way out of
the parking space and onto the pavement.

He drove slowly over the rain-slick streets, his weariness
too persistent now to ignore. The effects of this served also
to accent a growing feeling of discouragement over his lack
of progress. He was ready to admit that he had a better in-
sight into the characters and personalities of the people most
involved, but in terms of practical evidence that there had
been some collusion in a murder plan, he had nothing conclusive. He also understood that he had gone about as far
as he could without overstepping his authority, which was
limited at best. He could, when he got around to it the following day, pass along the information to Ballard. He could
outline his thoughts and ideas to the State's Attorney. There
the matter would have to stay unless he could convince
someone that the investigation should be continued and this
possibility, considered realistically, seemed unlikely.

He was still brooding about this lack of progress as he
turned into the alley behind his apartment. Here, on one
side, was a long row of wooden garages which were little
more than sheds with individual doors. Low-watt bulbs at
either end glowed weakly under hooded reflectors so that
the resulting light would not escape upward to disturb the
tenants of the adjacent apartment buildings.

Standish had to get out to open the doors before he could
drive in, and when he had taken the ignition key and closed
them he walked hurriedly back to the street. He turned

right here, coat collar still up and shoulders hunched against the light but steady drizzle. He turned right again at the corner, hugging the walls of the building for shelter. His own place was halfway down the block, and he walked hurriedly, bag in hand, as the shadows thickened. There were few windows lighted here at this hour and no sound except, somewhere up ahead, the low, pulsing throb of an idling motor.

Standish never knew what made him glance up, what made him stop so unaccountably just before he reached the glass doors of the apartment house. He was hurrying. His chin was tucked down against the rain. The sound of the motor meant nothing. Yet something, some inner compulsion, made him look up, and having done so he stopped short, not consciously but in response to an automatic and intuitive reflex he could not control.

Opposite the entrance and diagonally twenty feet away, in a no-parking zone marked by a yellow curb, stood this small sedan with the idling motor, the right-hand window rolled down and framing darkly a shadowed figure. Standish could not see it clearly. He was aware of a turned-up collar, a snap-brimmed felt hat hiding a half-seen face, the combined impression vague, because what caught his eye was the metallic glint at the end of an outthrust hand.

All this took but a fraction of a second, and it may have been the sudden stop that saved him. The expected step never came and as he stiffened the gun exploded. He saw the muzzle flash, and felt the lash of chips from the brick wall beside him. Then he was down, half diving, not toward the angle of the building but seeking the protection of another car parked at the curb, trying to pull his head behind his doctor's bag while the gun roared twice again in quick succession.

Later it came to him that he had moved in the right direction. By getting farther behind the gun he reduced the angle of fire but at no time did he look up. Taut-muscled

and immobile, he shrank there until he heard the motor ac-
celerate and the whine of gears. He lifted his head cau-
tiously as the sedan angled out from the curb with lights out
and license plate obscured. He did not even know what
kind of a car it was. Not new, he decided later, but fairly
new. And of a style that had been made almost universal
by automobile manufacturers, who seemed intent on making most of the inexpensive models look alike.

The moment he got to his feet he kept moving. He did
not want to be caught standing there while some curious
neighbor opened a window to find some answer for the
shots. Three long strides took him past the wet pavement
of the no-parking area. At the entrance he ducked quickly
inside. He met no one in the elevator but he was conscious
now of the tremor in his legs as reaction set in. He had a
little trouble with his door key, but once he was inside the
tension began to ease and his breathing became more
normal.

He put aside his bag and his topcoat and saw that his
trousers were wetly stained but not torn. The palms of his
hands were slick and grimy and when he had shucked his
jacket he went into the bathroom to wash them.

He was not sure when the trembling stopped. He soaked
and washed his hands. He dried them automatically and as
he caught his reflection in the mirror he found an odd grin
working on his eyes. This so amazed him that he wondered
why. When the answer finally came to him he accepted it
with satisfaction.

What up to now had been little more than a personal
hunch had suddenly taken on new significance. He had no
intention of bothering Lieutenant Ballard tonight, but tomorrow when he gave him the facts—there should be a bullet scar or two to substantiate his story—there was bound to
be some change in the official position. In addition, and this
seemed the most important of all, someone apparently was
getting pretty badly scared.

16

PAUL STANDISH was up early again on Thursday morning and as he drove to his office in the morgue he wondered when he would be able to resume his normal routine. It was too early for his secretary to put in an appearance but he knew that Clem Jones, the city chemist, usually arrived before anyone else. He left the outer door open and pulled up a chair so he could watch the hall and when, ten minutes later, Jones came in from the street, he stood up and beckoned.

"Hi, Doc," the chemist said. "Early, aren't you? You want to see me?"

He was a slender man of indeterminate age, with sharp features, inquisitive eyes, and thinning dark hair. He was a dedicated, underpaid public servant but he liked his work and seldom complained except when he wanted some new equipment not in the budget. Now, moving to the nearest desk, he watched while Standish opened his notebook to disclose the strand of hair he had taken from Donald Tremaine's divan.

"You can tell quite a lot about hair, can't you, Clem?"

"Yep," Jones said, his interest beginning to show as he bent to look at the specimen.

"Whether it's human or animal?"

"Yep. Unless you think it might have come from certain breeds of monkeys."

"Whether it's a man's or a woman's?"

"Usually. Also whether it's been bleached or dyed or had a recent permanent. What part of the body, et cetera, et cetera."

"Age group?"

"Relatively speaking."

"Could you tell whether this came from a particular person?"

"Nope. This one"—he indicated the specimen—"probably came from a woman's head unless maybe from one of those Beatle-type characters. Find me another one and I can tell you that maybe it did *not* come from the same head. If it shapes up as the same it could still come from some other woman."

"Okay. Do the best you can. I'll send you another specimen down later and you can make a comparison for me."

When Jones left, Standish telephoned Lou Cheney at his home. The answering voice sounded sleepy and mildly complaining about the early hour. Standish ignored the complaint and came to the point.

"Did you learn anything at Tremaine's last night?"

"A little something. He had a caller."

"When?"

"Not long after you left."

"Your man was there then? I didn't see him."

"If you had he wouldn't be working for me. . . . It was our brunette with the dark glasses. Off schedule, I guess, because according to the landlord she usually came on Sunday or Monday. Also this time she didn't stay but a half hour."

"Did you follow her?"

"We did. Do you want to guess where she went?"

Standish remembered the street address of Evelyn Tremaine's house and gave it.

"Right the first time," Cheney said.

Somehow the knowledge did not surprise Standish and he spoke of the other thing he had in mind.

"You've got keys that will open almost any door, haven't you?"

"We manage as a rule."

"I'd like to get into Evelyn Tremaine's house for about two minutes."

"What do you want there?"

"A hair."

"A what?" The inflection was incredulous. "You mean like on somebody's head?"

"From Mrs. Tremaine's head."

"How do you propose to get it? Stop her on the street and—"

Standish interrupted. "You go up to her bedroom and look around the vanity or her dressing table. You look at her hairbrush. How can you miss?"

"First tell me how you get in."

"Have you seen the house?"

"Sure."

"It's got high hedges on each side. There's no driveway from the street, which means that there must be an alley in the back leading to the garage. You put a man in a car down the street. When Mrs. Tremaine goes out—as she's bound to sometime—you go in the back way and in two minutes you're out again."

"I don't think so, Doc. Breaking and entering is a tough rap."

Standish had expected a refusal but he was determined now to get another specimen for Clem Jones and he suggested an alternative.

"Then do this, will you? Let me borrow your keys."

There was silence then and Standish let it go. He could hear, faintly, the sound of Cheney's breathing. After five seconds of this the detective answered.

"This must be awful important to you."

"It could be."

"Suppose," Cheney said, sounding very thoughtful, "that I case the joint and see what I can come up with."

"All you have to do is park down the street from the house. When Mrs. Tremaine goes out call my office. If I'm not there Mary'll know how to reach me. If I can get there before Mrs. Tremaine comes back, I'm willing to take a chance."

There was another pause but not quite so long as the first. Then Cheney said: "All right."

"You mean you'll let me have the keys?"

"No. If you're that determined I'll do it myself. But I'm going to throw a stipulation at you and you better think it over."

"What is it?"

"If I get caught, and I don't intend to, if they haul me in and ask me who I'm working for, I'm going to tell them. That means we're both up the creek."

"It's a deal," Standish said. "I'm not going to give it another thought because you're too good to get caught. When you get the hair take it down to Clem Jones at the morgue. He'll be in the second-floor laboratory. He expects it and he knows what to do. I'll be in touch later, Lou, and thanks."

Lieutenant Ballard met Paul Standish by appointment in front of his apartment house twenty minutes later. The phone call he had made from the morgue had been cryptic but insistent, and the idea behind his demand that this meeting take place here instead of in his office was due to the fact that he was not yet ready to have Mary Hayward worrying about what had happened the night before.

Ballard was using his own car as he moved into the curb in front of the apartment entrance and parked illegally. He looked very neat in his gray suit and light-colored raincoat, and his solid, good-looking face showed no traces of irritation as he asked what this was all about. Standish, who had already surveyed the scene, moved to the brick front of the building and pointed to a deep gouge where the surface had been chipped away. He let the lieutenant take a good look at the head-high mark, then indicated another similar pockmark lower down which apparently had been made when he had tried to throw himself flat.

"What do you think made these?" he asked.

Ballard's face grew somber and the gray eyes had a puzzled, watchful expression. "I might be able to guess if I knew why we were here. But you tell me if you know. What did make them?"

"Bullets," Standish said, and pointed at the sidewalk which showed an angular scar. "Three all told."

"When?"

"Last night," Standish said, and gave a detailed account of just what had happened after he had put his car in the garage. Ballard listened intently without interruption, his frown deepening. Once he re-examined the head-high scar on the wall and then he hunkered down to look at the other one. He dusted his palms, started to say something, and then waited until a woman wheeling a baby carriage had passed before he spoke.

"And you have no idea at all who fired the shots?"

"None."

"No license number."

"The car lights were out when I first noticed it."

"What kind of car?"

"Smallish, medium price, dark. Black or dark-gray or green."

"I mean what make?"

"I can't tell them apart any more unless I see the name or some emblem." Standish flipped one hand toward the sidewalk. "It was raining. I was flat, trying to hide behind my bag. I didn't stick my head out until I heard the car take off."

Ballard kicked at a cigarette butt on the sidewalk and seemed at a loss for words. A dispassionate appraisal of his

attitude should have told Standish that the lieutenant was
troubled by what had happened, that his glumness arose
from his inability to explain the incident, that he was all too
aware that it was no longer possible to brush aside the doctor's theory.

When he neglected to say so, Standish crowded him:
"This one you can't hang on Ralph Estey."

Ballard eyed him fretfully. "Okay. So maybe you've got
an idea who we *can* hang it on."

Standish shrugged. "I tried to tell you what I thought
once before."

"I remember. You wanted to explain the whys and where-
fores of vehicular homicide. You had some idea that maybe
Flemming was hired to run down Robert Tremaine. Flemming got away with it and you think he got greedy and
wanted a second payment and this somebody fed him
chloral hydrate and then shot him."

"Someone," Standish said, "who knew about that fight
Friday night and the threats that Estey had made about the
gun. By setting up Estey as a suicide he figured you might
wrap it up that way and you did."

"On the face of it we had no choice." Ballard tipped his
head, gray eyes half closed now and his suspicion showing.
"Maybe you have got something we haven't. Have you been
talking to the widow and the ex-partner and—"

"I've been doing a little talking, yes. I might be able to
give you a motive or two. If they make any sense you can
do some checking of your own."

"Good enough. Suppose you come down to Headquarters. We'll go over this thing again, bit by bit and piece by
piece."

"That's a fine idea now that you've got an open mind."
Standish grinned to take the sting out of his words and
said: "But it will have to wait a while, Tom. I've got to get

to the office and I have some house calls to make. It may be around noon but I'll do the best I can."

The offices of Choate & Tremaine occupied part of the mezzanine floor of the City National Bank. Two glass doors bearing the firm's name gave on a large reception room with a counter at one end. The area beyond was cut into offices by wood-and-glass partitions but there were none of the usual trappings one expected to find in a brokerage house—no wall-to-wall quotation board, no illuminated Translux tape, no rows of customers' chairs. This was no place for the day trader because the firm had a rather specialized clientele.

Choate did not have a seat on the New York Stock Exchange. He operated through a correspondent and could buy and sell for clients in the customary way. It took longer to get quotes over the telephone but this was no great drawback since the bulk of the business was in new issues or secondary distributions, and in municipal bonds. Paul Standish, arriving at eleven-thirty with his house calls taken care of, stepped to the counter, gave his name, and said he would like to see Warren Choate on a personal matter. The girl at the small switchboard flipped a key, spoke briefly, glanced up, and gestured to a closed door on the right.

Warren Choate's private office was smallish and comfortable but more utilitarian than luxurious. He did not rise from behind his desk when Standish entered and closed the door, and his tan, muscular face was hostile, his manner abrupt.

"This is one of my busy days, Doctor," he said. "What is it this time?"

"It won't take long," Standish said. "Does Donald Tremaine have an account with you?"

"He does."

"I'd like to know if you made a transaction for him in December."

"Why don't you ask him?"

"Because he could say anything he wanted to. To be sure I'd have to consult the records. You have them."

"They are also confidential. You ought to know that. Without Donald's consent I couldn't give you that information. If you want to see the records you'd better get yourself a subpoena, Doctor."

Standish met the rebuff without rancor. His voice remained calm, confident, and explicit, even though what he said was mostly bluff.

"Whatever you say, Mr. Choate." He sat on the arm of the chair and took his time. "You may have heard that I talked to your wife and Mrs. Tremaine yesterday afternoon."

"I heard all right. They resented it and so do I. In fact I think Mrs. Tremaine is consulting her attorney now."

"That's all right," Standish said. "That's her privilege. But I can tell you now that something happened last night that knocked a hole in the police theory that Ralph Estey killed Flemming and then committed suicide. I wouldn't be surprised if you got a call from Lieutenant Ballard later in the day and I don't think he'll have any trouble getting a subpoena. Of course, the minute he does, the newspapers will have it. If you'd rather have that publicity than tell me in private—well, that's up to you." He rose, straightened his jacket, and was almost to the door before Choate stopped him.

"Just a minute."

Standish waited, hopes rising but trying to keep his face expressionless. For another second or two the man eyed him with cold distaste but when he spoke there was a trace of uncertainty in his voice.

"What, exactly, is it that you want to know?"

Standish considered the date of the accident and said: "I want to know what, if anything, you bought or sold for Don-

ald Tremaine between December fifth and December nine-
teenth."

Choate hesitated, glanced away. Finally he put both
palms flat on the desk and stood up. He straightened his
shoulders and then started round the desk, saying that he
would see what he could find. Standish walked over to the
window, aware now of the strain he felt and grinning a little
in his relief. He wiped his palms with his handkerchief and
was waiting with cigarette in hand when Choate returned,
a worried look on his face and a manila folder in his hand.
He opened the folder on his desk and selected an oblong
printed form. He looked at it once more, put it back.

"We sold a hundred shares of American Factories for
Donald on December ninth at fifty-one and a quarter."

"That would amount to around five thousand," Standish
said.

"A little over, net."

"Did you credit his account or give him a check or cash
or what?"

Choate sat down again, his gaze fixed on the window. "I
remember now," he said. "He wanted cash. It wasn't actually due because the settlement date is not the day of the
sale, but there was no reason why we shouldn't accommo-
date him. We wrote out a check for the records and he sat
right there while I sent a boy downstairs to get the cash."

Standish said *"Ah-h!"* silently as a surge of satisfaction
came over him. Aloud he said: "Thank you very much, Mr.
Choate."

Again he was nearly to the door when Choate stopped
him.

"Were you serious about the police?"

"I'm afraid I was," Standish said. "I have an idea someone may stop by before the day is over. They'll probably
ask a lot more questions than I did."

17

THE DOOR of Ballard's little office stood open and there was no one in the outer room when Paul Standish walked in just after twelve to find the lieutenant at his desk, chin down and a brooding look in his gray eyes. He let Standish sit down without comment and his opening remark was gruffly critical but not unfriendly.

"You took your time getting here."

"People get sick." Standish grinned. "They need my expert and kindly attention."

Ballard's grunt was noncommittal but he finally pushed erect in his chair and reached for a cigarette. "Okay," he said when he had a light, "tell me about your theory on vehicular homicide."

Standish understood that this was just Ballard's way of getting to more important things, but he complied with the request, quoting past examples in which an automobile had been used as an instrument of death, not only with homicidal intent but as a vehicle of suicide.

"We've been able to prove it on one or two occasions. We suspect it in many others but it still goes on the books as another traffic accident."

Ballard listened without comment and his brooding look became less noticeable. "So," he said finally, "let's assume you're right about Flemming and Robert Tremaine. Who do you think stood to gain the most by his death?"

Standish spoke of the insurance policies and how they were payable. When Ballard began to take notes he mentioned Robert Tremaine's personal estate and the trust fund which he controlled for Donald Tremaine.

F

"In other words," Ballard said, "our friend Donald would have had to wait nearly two years to collect if his brother hadn't been killed. So what have we got in the money way?" He consulted his figures. "The widow got a hundred grand from the company insurance, eighty more from the double-indemnity personal policies, and something like a hundred from her husband's personal estate. . . . Choate owns the business. . . . Donald, assuming the trust fund is about the same size as his brother's personal estate, got about the same as the widow—say two hundred and eighty thousand. . . . Hmmm," he added, sounding impressed. "That's a lot of scratch."

"Also," Standish said, "there's a more personal element that could shape up as a possible motive. The Choates are divorcing. Apparently they had already decided to call it quits before the accident. Mrs. Choate has a prospective husband in New York all ready and waiting for the final decree. Choate seems to have a thing going with Evelyn Tremaine. That also could have started sometime before the accident."

"Yeah. Well." Ballard stopped and his eyes opened. "How the hell do you know all that? Where'd you get it?"

Standish gave a small shrug and considered his reply. He was not ready yet to speak of Lou Cheney and his activities because this, as Mary Hayward had pointed out, was in the realm of extracurricular activity that might be a little hard to justify. On the other hand he was more than willing to pass along the information he had because this was something that could have been done by the police.

"I talked to people," he said.

"What people?"

"The people we've just mentioned. You could have done the same thing if you hadn't been so sold on the murder-suicide idea. I couldn't buy it, so I decided to do a little snooping on my own. You can double-check it—"

"And don't think we won't," Ballard said. "You got anything else that might help?"

"Well—Jess Flemming seemed a little more prosperous right after that accident."

"We know about that."

"And you might want to ask Donald Tremaine why he sold five thousand dollars' worth of stock on December ninth. And what he did with the money."

Ballard made another note and Standish said: "You brushed aside the chloral hydrate finding—"

"I didn't brush it aside," Ballard said with some indignation. "I merely said there were other ways to figure it."

"The paraffin test was negative."

"And don't think that didn't bother me," Ballard said. "I still say the test itself is not conclusive and wouldn't stand up in court, but I kept asking myself the same question you did—how could Estey fire that gun without having some powder traces on his hand? But I'm not the boss around here. Cavanaugh was ready to buy the obvious and the State's Attorney's office wasn't ready to make a move without additional evidence. Now maybe we can get some."

While Ballard had been talking Standish stood up to put out his cigarette. There was an oblong table which stood along the wall behind Ballard's chair and when Standish used the ashtray he noticed a wire basket containing a large manila envelope. Beneath this and partly hidden was a short-barreled revolver and he leaned closer to read the name that had been typed on the envelope.

"Is this Estey's stuff?"

"In the envelope, yes."

"Is this the gun? All right to look at it?"

Ballard said yes and Standish picked up the gun, noting the tag which had been attached to the trigger guard. He flipped out the cylinder, flipped it back. He balanced it in his palm and as he did so he saw the manufacturer's trademark imprinted on the black composition stock. The two initials in the circle were a capital S and a capital W.

His glance started to move on and something pulled it back. An instant later the dark-blue eyes were brightly intent as his mind reversed itself. He retreated to his chair with the gun still in his palm and suddenly he was back in Hennessey's and it was Friday night and he was seated across the table from Ralph Estey talking about jazz and musicians, trumpet players in particular. Afterward he had spoken of Estey's threat. He remembered distinctly what the man had said. Now, glancing up, he saw that Ballard was watching him narrowly and there must have been something showing in his face because the lieutenant said:

"What's the matter?"

"Is this the gun you found in the musicians' room?"

"Sure. Why?"

"It wasn't there when I came in," Standish said slowly in his concentration. "I asked you about it and you said it was a .32 and you had dug the bullet out of the wall. You had an idea it was the same gun he used on Flemming."

"And it was," Ballard said. "Ballistics proved it."

"A Smith and Wesson."

"Right."

"I talked some with Ralph Estey Friday night after the fight," Standish said, and repeated the pertinent sentences. "I heard the threat and I asked Ralph if he really had a gun. He said he did. He said it was an old H & R."

"H & R?" Ballard shook his head. "Harrington and Richardson?" He drew the words out, a look of puzzlement in his eyes. "He must have got it twisted."

"Why should he?" Standish asked. "You couldn't have a gun a long time without knowing what kind it was. If it was a Harrington and Richardson you'd know it. You could say it was an H & R but you wouldn't mistake it for a Smith and Wesson, would you?"

Ballard extended his hand and Standish put the gun in his palm. He watched the lieutenant inspect it, saw the deepening frown and look of uncertainty as Ballard finally laid the weapon aside.

"He could have been mistaken," he said stubbornly.

"You could ask his ex-wife, couldn't you?"

"How would she know?"

"I don't say she would," Standish said evenly. "But if Ralph had that gun as long as he said he did, and he was married for eight or ten years, she must have seen it; probably several times."

"Just the same—" Ballard was not quite ready to give up but Standish interrupted.

"If the H & R was a similar model to this Smith and Wesson she probably wouldn't know the difference. But if it had a longer barrel or different type of action she ought to be able to tell whether this is the same or not."

He stopped, tired of talking and having no further suggestions. "Do what you want to," he said, heading for the door. "Ralph said he had an H & R. I'll take an oath on that. You got an S & W. You figure it."

To save time Standish sat on a stool at a drugstore counter and had a sandwich and a milkshake, and it was ten minutes to one when he stepped into his reception room to find Evelyn Tremaine talking to Mary Hayward. Apparently the woman had just arrived, since both were standing, and Mary said "Here he is now" as soon as she saw him.

Evelyn examined him with humid dark eyes as he said "Good afternoon" and put aside his bag. She wore a smooth-fitting navy dress and a mink jacket, and the impression she gave was expensive, superior, poised, and impatient. Yet even as he heard her throaty voice asking to see him in private he thought of other things and wondered what this woman would be like once the veneer—and he thought it was a veneer—of aloofness was stripped away.

He motioned her toward his consulting room and opened the door, nodding to Mary and indicating the telephone on her desk. Once inside, he surreptitiously switched on his inter-com as he asked the woman to be seated.

She began by stating flatly that she had come to make a threat. She was aware, she said, of the inquiries he had made of her brother-in-law and Warren Choate; furthermore, the insinuations he had made the day before had so upset her that she had consulted her attorney, who assured her that Dr. Standish had neither the authority nor the legal right to undertake such an investigation. She said if he persisted in such unwarranted insinuations she and the others involved would see that the matter was placed before the proper authorities.

Standish let her finish, knowing that she had reasonable grounds for her promised action even as his mind went on to other things. He wondered if the woman had been out earlier or if Lou Cheney was at this moment looking over her bedroom for a sample of her hair. He considered again the information he had forced from Warren Choate and took satisfaction in the thought that Ballard would now be working on his side. He watched her straighten her jacket and said he would like to ask a question.

"You went to see Donald Tremaine last night, I believe?"

Something flickered in the dark depths of her eyes and was gone. "Perhaps."

"You've visited him at his place other times as well."

Again something happened to her eyes, but the look was veiled before he could fathom it. She flicked a piece of lint off her dress and when she glanced up her smile was studied.

"Visited Donald?" she said with mild hauteur. "Since my husband's death? Don't be ridiculous, Doctor."

She stood up then and Standish rose with her.

"I appreciate your warning, Mrs. Tremaine," he said. "And you won't have to worry about me any more. Any further investigation will be done by the police. They have the necessary authority and they will probably use it."

Mary came in as soon as the outer door closed. "She'll do it, Doctor," she said. "She'll make trouble for you."

Standish's smile was slow and understanding, because he sensed her anxiety and knew her concern was for him.

"Maybe," he said, "but I doubt it."

Mary gave a little hopeless shake of her head. There was no censure in her manner now. She was worried about him and it showed in her young face.

"I wish you'd tell me what you've been doing, and why," she wailed. "You've talked to me before when you've had problems. If I only knew what was happening and what you were trying to do—"

"You will, Mary," Standish said. He took her by the elbow and gently turned her toward the door. "Just as soon as the office is clear. There should be someone out there now. Do you want to take a look?"

18

IT TOOK nearly three hours for Paul Standish to handle his regular appointments and three others that came unannounced and had to be taken care of. When at last the outer office was empty, Mary came into the consulting room, leaving the door open. She slumped wearily in the chair opposite the desk, and Standish, knowing what she wanted, had just begun to talk when the telephone rang. She answered it, spoke briefly.

"Clem Jones," she said.

"Hi, Clem," Standish said. "Did Cheney show up with

that other specimen? . . . Good enough. So? . . . Yeah."
Then, with a quickened cadence: "Dyed? You're sure? It's
what? . . . No. That's okay. Just hang on to them—and
thanks."

Not looking at Mary, he depressed the bar to break the
connection and then dialed Lou Cheney's number. After a
few rings the operator for the answering service came on
and he left a message for Cheney to call him as soon as
possible.

When he hung up and leaned back in his chair Mary
asked no questions but her gray eyes were pleading for information and he resumed his story where he had left off.
To justify certain actions he knew he had to tell her about
what had happened outside his apartment house the night
before, and even though he minimized the danger he could
see that she was frightened and distressed. An unaccus-
tomed pallor had crept into her cheeks and her mouth was
slack when he finished.

"Oh, no," she said, her voice hushed. "Why? Because
someone thought you were getting too close to the truth?"

"Probably."

"And you didn't see who it was?"

"No."

"Did you tell the lieutenant?"

"This morning. He met me out front of my place. I talked
with him again later."

"What does he think? What's he going to do about it?"

"I imagine he's taking it up where I left off."

He went on to relate the details of his talk with Donald
Tremaine and Warren Choate. He spoke of the stock sale
Tremaine had made three days before the accident and his
demand for cash.

"You mean that might have been how he paid Flemming?
But"—she gave a small distracted gasp—"it all seems so hor-
rible. It was bad enough for Flemming to run down Robert
Tremaine—even if, as you say, he was the kind of man who

might do a thing like that. But then to shoot him and that poor Ralph Estey—I mean it's so cold-blooded."

"Right," Standish said. "Flemming had become a menace. He had to be removed. He was the type who couldn't be threatened or scared off. A man like that could only be handled in one way. I guess if you were desperate enough it wouldn't be too hard. Estey was just a poor patsy who could make the murder-suicide theory stand up."

Mary leaned forward in her chair, lips still parted and eyes enormous. "Do you know who it was, Paul?" she said, forgetting to be formal.

"I've got an idea but—"

The telephone shrilled an interruption before he could finish.

"Maybe that's Cheney," he said. But when Mary answered she shook her head. "The lieutenant."

"Doc?" Ballard said. "Just wanted to tell you you were right."

Standish made no reply and the silence built until Ballard broke it.

"Did you hear what I said?"

"Yes. In what way was I right?"

"About the gun. I showed it to Estey's ex-wife. She says no."

"Does she know anything about guns?"

"Not much. But she's seen Estey's enough to give me a rough description. She says the barrel was a little longer. And Estey must have been right about it being an old gun because she said the cylinder didn't flip out like the Smith and Wesson. It was a tip-up action. You know, you have to break it to load or eject shells. You want to figure the rest of this for me or shall I tell you how it looks to me?"

"You sound as if you're buying my theory now."

"I have to. What the hell else can I do? The way it looks to me, that Smith and Wesson is the kind of gun a guy like Flemming would own. Someone walked in on him—someone he knew—and had a couple of drinks and slipped him the chloral hydrate just like you said when you got the pathologist's report. When Flemming passes out our boy looks around for a gun—Flemming might even have been carrying it—and uses it. He takes it with him—"

"He'd have to know about the fight Friday night and Estey's threat," Standish said.

"Sure. But that could apply to any of the people you've been talking to. The same people would know that Hennessey's is closed Monday nights. It wouldn't be too hard to con Estey into some kind of meeting in that musicians' room. Estey had a key to the place and our boy would know the body wouldn't be discovered until probably Tuesday evening. Somebody brings a pint and they have a drink and the guy uses the gun."

Ballard swore softly and said: "That poor bastard probably never knew what happened. . . . Anyway, the guy had to use the Smith and Wesson because to make the murder-suicide thing stand up the two slugs had to match. He left that gun and probably took the Harrington and Richardson that Estey said he would be carrying. He probably still has it."

"He probably," Standish said, "used it on me last night."

"Sure. Well—I just wanted to tell you how it looks from here. Now that we know which way we're moving we ought to come up with something before too long."

"Where'll you be later?" Standish asked.

"Working. If I'm not here they'll know where to reach me. You think of anything else, give me a buzz, okay?"

Standish passed along the information to Mary but it was nearly six before Lou Cheney returned his call.

"What's it this time, Doc?" the detective asked, coming straight to the point.

"Clem Jones called me. He said you delivered. No trouble at the widow's?"

"No. Didn't expect any. It was simple enough except that

I don't like to operate that way. If I hadn't known you quite
a while I'd have said no and stuck to it."

"Have you still got a man on Donald Tremaine?"

"Pulled him off this morning. But he came up with a little
something first, probably not important."

"What?"

"On his way to the office, Tremaine stopped at the downtown air terminal and made some inquiries about flight
times and fares to Miami and Panama. He didn't buy any
tickets."

The information quickened Standish's interest and gave
substance to the idea he already had in mind.

"Good enough, Lou. And look—I think I can afford a few
more hours of your time. Could you put a man on Tremaine's place this evening? The one who was there last
night if he's free."

"When?"

"Well—just as soon as it gets dark."

"What are you after?"

"I just want to see if he has any visitors."

"Like maybe the brunette friend?"

"Something like that—I hope."

"Where'll you be?"

"Right here in my office. If anyone shows, have your man
phone me here. If nothing happens by midnight he can call
it off."

Mary had been listening intently to every word, the gray
eyes round and the lips slightly parted. She watched him
cradle the telephone, the impatience growing in her.

"What," she demanded when he made no comment, "are
you going to do if this visitor does come?"

"Pay Tremaine a little call." Standish sat up and glanced
at his watch. "It's getting late," he said. "Why don't you run
along?"

"How will you eat?"

"You can get me a sandwich and coffee before you leave."

She eyed him steadily for a moment or two and then stood up. She moved past the desk and on through the examining room to the dressing room. When she came back she was wearing a tailored green dress and her camel's-hair coat. "What kind? Ham, cheese, chicken, tuna-fish—"

"Chicken, I guess. With plenty of coffee."

When she went out Standish hoisted himself out of his chair and went into the examining room to get some ice. He poured a good-sized drink and was nearly finished when Mary returned with three brown-paper bags. From the first she produced two sandwiches, one of which she placed in front of him and the other across the desk by the patient's chair. From the second she took two large cartons of coffee, and from the third came two fresh pears and a bunch of seedless grapes.

She unwrapped the sandwiches and produced paper napkins. She got two cups from the examining room and some little envelopes containing sugar. Standish waited until she sat down. He examined his sandwich. When Mary finally looked at him he smiled.

"So," he said, "you won't go home."

"No. This time I'm going to stay. I'm going wherever you go. If you get into trouble I want to know about it."

She picked up half her sandwich, her gaze challenging and defiant. Standish, some part of his mind already grateful for her attitude, eyed her fondly. "Let's eat," he said, "I'm hungry."

"Me too." She took a determined bite of her sandwich. "I hope you like grapes."

And so they ate and made the coffee last as long as they could and smoked cigarettes and turned on the office radio. There was a tiny portable television set here but there was nothing on they wanted to see. Standish tried to interest himself in one of the recent medical journals and Mary pretended to be absorbed in a paperback novel which she had produced from her handbag. They said very little and both seemed conscious of the desk clock, which crept with discouraging slowness to eight-thirty, to nine, to nine-thirty. Finally, with an explosion of sound that startled them both, the telephone rang.

Standish did not recognize the voice which came to him, but the message was clear.

"Right," he said. "Stay there! I'm on my way."

19

PAUL STANDISH found the man in the shadows diagonally across the street after he had parked his sedan a hundred feet short of the narrow-front house where Donald Tremaine lived. Here in the darkness he was a plump, fairly short man, with no identifying features showing under the hat brim but a straight mouth and a solid-looking chin.

"Unless she moved right out again while I was calling you"—the detective pointed toward a corner filling station a block and a half away—"she's still up there."

"The same one that was here last night?"

"I wouldn't want to swear to it. I almost missed her. If she came in a car she left it on the other street. She was walking, just turning in, when I spotted her. Dark dress, dark glasses, dark coat."

"Do you know anything about the other tenants?"

"Top floor"—he pointed to the lighted front windows—"a young couple. Name of Carney. Third floor"—here the windows were dark—"an older couple named Walker. They turned out the light just before I phoned. Probably went to bed. The landlord lives alone."

A car rolled past as he was talking and when Standish

started to speak he felt the hand on his arm and stopped. The hand moved, pointing now, and Standish saw that the car had pulled into the curb just short of the corner. They waited that way, immobile and silent, while the car lights went out. Finally there came the light but unmistakable tapping of heels on the opposite sidewalk. Only the sound marked the woman's progress until she was almost opposite the entrance and Standish had only a quick glance before she turned and was inside.

What he saw was another woman who could have fitted the detective's previous description. Dark hair, dark glasses, dark coat. The only difference was that this woman—he was quite sure of this—wore a scarf on her head.

The detective grunted softly. "Unless she's calling on the landlord or the Carneys, it looks like this Tremaine is a popular guy. . . . Do you want anything more from me?"

Standish had nothing in mind but, not knowing what would happen next, he was reluctant to let the man go.

"Where's your car?"

The detective pointed to the next intersection. "Round the corner, a tan Chevvy sedan."

"Do you think you can locate the car this last woman came in? . . . Then get the license number and wait in your Chevvy."

"What are you going to do?" Mary said when the man moved on. "Shouldn't you call Lieutenant Ballard?"

It was a good question and Standish found some irony in the situation when he realized that Mary, who normally wanted nothing to do with Ballard, was now suggesting that he be asked for some support.

"I've been thinking about it for quite a while," he said.

"Are you going up there?"

"Yes. And at this point I think I'd better go alone."

"Why?"

"I know a thing or two that Ballard doesn't. The trouble is what I have is not conclusive and may prove nothing.

Ballard has to go by the book. He has to observe certain rules and regulations, especially the way the courts are looking at things these days. I can go up there as an individual with nothing to lose."

"Except your reputation."

"But I do think," he added, ignoring the interruption, "that Ballard ought to know about this. Will you walk down to that filling station and call him?"

"Well—all right," Mary said with some reluctance. "But what do I say?"

"Tell him where I am. Tell him I have a lead that he might want to look into. If he comes to Tremaine's and asks for me I don't think he'll be breaking any regulations."

Mary did not like it; her voice said so. "And what will you be doing?"

Standish was not quite sure as he moved off in the darkness without bothering to reply. He had an idea he could get more information out of Tremaine than Ballard could officially, and having come this far practically alone, he had to try. He told himself this as he stood on the second-floor landing and knocked on Tremaine's door, then knocked again, while the tension began to build slowly inside him.

It was a good five seconds before there was a reply, and then a man's voice said: "Who is it?"

"Dr. Standish."

Another few seconds went by. Finally a lock clicked and the door opened about a foot, framing Tremaine's bespectacled face.

"I'm sorry, Doctor," he said in his formal way. "I have company."

"I know. That's what I want to talk to you about."

Standish was moving as he spoke, putting his weight against the door swiftly and with precision, forcing the smaller man back, then pushing into the room.

He saw the woman sitting in the easy chair by the window as the door slammed behind him. Then Tremaine, in slacks and sport shirt but impeccably groomed as always, darted in front of him, the jaw hard now and the mouth white with rage.

"You can't come in here like this," he yelled. "Not even the police can come in here without a warrant. Either you leave at once or I'll call them now."

"Why don't you? That might be a good idea."

Standish spoke quietly and it was apparent that he meant what he said. He was not looking at Tremaine. He had not looked at him since he had entered. Instead his attention had focused on Evelyn Tremaine. Her coat had been thrown back. The dark glasses and the scarf were in her lap. The sleek black hair glistened in the lamplight and the dark eyes were intent and challenging.

Donald Tremaine put a hand on Standish's shoulder and pulled forcefully, half turning him. The anger was still gripping the smaller man and he stood spread-legged, fists at his side. For a second or two he seemed about to swing and then the moment passed.

"What do you want?" he demanded.

"For one thing," Standish said, "I'd like to ask Mrs. Tremaine a couple of questions."

"How did you know she was here? If you've been following her—"

The woman cut him off. "Let it go, Donald. I think I'd like to hear the questions."

Standish straightened his coat collar. He was reasonably sure of his ground now but he wanted confirmation.

"Do you dye your hair, Mrs. Tremaine?"

"I do not."

"You haven't had any recent permanent either, have you?"

"Not since I was a teen-ager. How do you know?"

"I picked up a strand when I was at your place yesterday," Standish lied, having no intention of involving Lou Cheney. "I had an expert examine it. He said no dye, no

permanent. You were here last night. This afternoon I asked
you a question. I'll ask it again. I'd like the truth because
the clock is beginning to run out on all of you."

"In what way?"

"The police have changed their minds. They're convinced
now that the Flemming-Estey case was not murder and suicide but a very clever plot. They agree that there could be
only one reason for such a plot—that Flemming was hired
to run down your husband in a deliberate murder attempt."

Behind him Tremaine was protesting in outraged tones
but the woman did not bat an eye. "What was your question?"

"I asked if you'd been here to see Donald regularly, prior
to last night. You said no."

"Because it happens to be the truth."

This time Standish believed her. He took a small breath,
not liking what he had to do but knowing no other way.
With one eye on Tremaine he moved quickly to the inner
hall, continuing to a sizable bedroom with twin beds, a
maple chest and dresser. There was an adjoining bath and
a closed door apparently giving on a closet.

Once again as he started forward Tremaine ducked in
front of him, his bespectacled face white and stiff, his voice
raging.

"God damn you, Standish!" he said. "I told you to get
out."

And then, having spoken, he swung. It was not an artful
blow but it was unexpected and he gave it all he had. Standish saw it coming and had time to jerk his head, not quite
enough, but enough to vitiate its force.

As it was, the punch grazed his cheekbone and he went
back a step, and Tremaine was after him swinging a left.
The trouble was, Standish had done some boxing in college
and Tremaine apparently had not, and now the left was
neatly slipped and Standish was inside, trapping the arm
and shifting his weight. He did not strike Tremaine; he

merely spun him off his feet and dumped him against the edge of the nearest bed, from which he bounced to the floor.

In that same instant he reached for the closet door and yanked and then he was face to face with the woman. The dark coat was over one arm, the handbag dangling from the other wrist. She still had the dark glasses on and the black bobbed hair did not fool him now. He recognized the simple dark dress with the white collar and somehow he felt no great surprise.

"All right, Sheila," he said. "Do you want to take the wig off or shall I?"

All this took perhaps five seconds and during that time no one else spoke. Then Tremaine jumped up and gave vent to his feelings. He said he'd have Standish arrested; he'd have his license revoked. He said other things as Standish heard him out.

"If I were you," he said when it was all over, "I'd do some listening."

He had not taken his eyes from Sheila Keith and now he watched her take the glasses off and fold them. She removed the black wig with some care and shook out the ash-blond hair. The familiar smile which was her stock in trade was absent now and the green eyes were bright and hard in the set white face.

Standish stepped back to let her move into the room and he saw that Evelyn Tremaine, apparently alerted by the sound of the commotion, was standing in the doorway to the bedroom. Her dark beauty had a strained look now and her glance moved to Tremaine and to Standish before settling on Sheila Keith.

"So it's you," she said quietly.

She turned and went back into the living room and Standish motioned Sheila Keith ahead of him. Tremaine, after a brief attack of speechlessness, found his voice when he came back to the front room.

"I'd better call the police," he said, heading toward the telephone as he spoke. He took two steps before Sheila Keith stopped him.

"Wait a minute, Don!" Her voice was clipped, commanding. "Let him talk."

Tremaine hesitated, wavered, obeyed. Evelyn Tremaine had gone back to her chair. Sheila Keith took the matching one across from the fireplace, wig, glasses, and handbag in her lap. Standish perched on the arm of the divan and looked at Tremaine.

"I guess you're in love with her."

"Certainly I'm in love with her."

"That might explain your inquiries yesterday morning at the downtown airline's office. Miami and Panama, wasn't it? For a honeymoon?"

"Suppose it was?"

"When?"

"None of your damn business."

"But you've been in love for quite a while, haven't you? Since before your brother was killed? . . . Then why didn't you marry her? Why wait? Or was it Sheila who did the stalling? Maybe, until that accident, you weren't just what she had in mind for a husband. You didn't have much of a job, you didn't have much money. You couldn't get any for two years until you had control of that trust fund."

"Or," he added when there was no immediate reply, "was it because your brother, who apparently dominated you the same way your father did, might make trouble if he knew about you and Sheila?"

The rage in Tremaine had passed. What anger remained now was under control and his resentment showed only in the pale patches along the cheekbone and in the overtones of his voice.

"It's still none of your business what I did or what Sheila did."

"Maybe," Standish said, "but unless you've got a very good story to tell the police you'll probably face murder charges; at least, you'll wind up as an accessory."

Tremaine leaned forward, jaw slack and widely staring. He seemed to have trouble answering and when the words came they were uncertain.

"I don't know what you're talking about."

"You could be right," Standish said, "but it's time you found out."

He went on quickly then, his voice quiet, assured, and intent. He reminded Tremaine of their previous talk the evening before and the doubt he had expressed about Robert Tremaine's accidental death. He outlined the theory again, adding that it was no longer theory but fact. Then quickly he said: "You got five thousand dollars in cash from Warren Choate three days before that accident."

"He sold some stock for me."

"Yes. But he said a check wasn't good enough for you. He had to send down and have it cashed. . . . What did you do with it?" he pressed when Tremaine did not reply. "Who did you give it to?"

Tremaine had been standing in front of the fireplace. Now he braced his shoulders against the edge of the mantelpiece and folded his arms. He stuck his chin out and his bespectacled gaze was steady and defiant.

"Go to hell!"

"You mean that's none of my business either? You could be right about that," Standish said. "But once the police find out about that transaction—and for all I know they already have—they're going to make it their business. If you want to know what they're going to say, I'll tell you," he added, and went on before he could be interrupted.

"When they find out about Sheila—and you can be damn sure I'm going to tell them—and realize that you had a thing going here every Sunday or Monday night—the only nights she was free when you stop to think of it—they are going to say you planned that accident to your brother because it was the only way you could get Sheila. You were in love with her. You wanted to marry her. She wouldn't have you with what you had but there was a trust fund that could be yours and your brother was holding out. You were going to get one half of the company insurance and one half of the personal insurance. Add it all up and it comes to more than a quarter of a million dollars."

He took a breath and said: "What else are they going to think? It fits. All of it. You had to get your brother out of the way—you probably hated him anyway—and you didn't have the nerve to do it yourself because the police could pin too many motives on you. But somewhere along the line you found out about a guy named Jess Flemming. You knew his background. You knew he could be hired. You knew your brother's habits, especially his drinking habits on Saturday nights. It wouldn't be too tough to set up. For five thousand Flemming agreed to do the job, so you sold the stock—"

Tremaine interrupted, a rising desperation in his tone. "But it's not true. That's not the way it happened."

"You're going to have to tell the police why you needed that five thousand dollars. Why hold out on us? What are you afraid of? We can't arrest you."

Evelyn Tremaine, who had been watching intently, shifted her legs and cleared her throat. "Why *did* you need that five thousand, Donald?"

"Why?" Tremaine's glance shifted behind the spectacles and came back. "For Sheila."

"You gave it to her?" Evelyn Tremaine said in slow astonishment. "Just like that?"

"In cash?" Standish said.

"She wanted cash."

"Why?"

"To pay off a mortgage on her mother's home. She supported her mother—out in Ohio. She said she couldn't marry me with that mortgage over her head."

Standish let his breath out slowly. Something about the other's manner, his almost naïve sincerity, told him that this must be the truth. A moment later, and remembering what Marion Choate and Evelyn had told him, he understood why.

"Ingenuous" was one of the words they had used to describe Tremaine. With women, they said, he had no experience. With this in mind it was easy to see how malleable and unsuspecting he might be when someone like Sheila Keith decided she wanted him. Sheila had been around. She had been married and there had no doubt been others since then.

Her background in the entertainment business had given her a working understanding of what made most men tick. She had both the practice and the experience to please them when necessary. In the past months on her Sunday or Monday night visits, she had undoubtedly given Tremaine something he had never had before. He had apparently taken her physical attraction and cooperation for love and, glancing at him now, it seemed to Standish that Tremaine was still sold on the girl.

"A mortgage?" he said. "Sheila told me her mother was dead but that's something we can check. Now, let me tell you what I think she did with that five thousand. She gave it to Jess Flemming. Flemming was for hire if the price was right and the risk reasonable and"—he nodded toward the girl—"she knew it. She'd known him before. She knew all about him."

He said: "She wouldn't marry you while your brother was alive, would she? What did she tell you?" He expected no answer and continued quickly: "Whatever her excuse, she spent enough time here with you to know all about the insurance policies, and the double indemnity, and the trust fund that you wouldn't get for two more years. She could add. With your brother dead she had what she wanted. For all I know she may have planned to have Mrs. Tremaine killed at the same time; that would make you even more desirable. If she did, Flemming missed Evelyn, and anyway it doesn't matter now."

Tremaine wet his lips. He shook his head, his eyes incredulous. "You were saying that Sheila hired Flemming to kill my brother?" he asked in hushed tones.

"That's exactly what I'm saying. She gave you the con about the mortgage in Ohio and you got the five thousand for her. She gave it to Flemming and Flemming did the job. My testimony about your brother's drunken condition helped get Flemming off. He took the money and went West. He had himself a time and bought a car and when he came back he started to pester Sheila.

"In the beginning I think she convinced him that she was acting for someone else. Later, with his money about gone, I think he got suspicious. I think he may have followed her on one of her Sunday or Monday night visits. Once he found out about you it wouldn't be hard to figure why Sheila wanted your brother killed accidentally. You had already collected and she was going to marry you when the time was right. But Flemming was on a spot to do some collecting himself. When he told her so, she knew she had to kill him or he'd bleed her to death. . . ."

He stopped abruptly, held by some new change in Tremaine. The gaze had shifted and the bespectacled eyes had a funny expression. He said: "No, Sheila!" And there was something in the cadence of that voice that made the hairs on the back of Standish's neck prickle coldly.

He turned slowly. He looked at Sheila Keith. Then he saw the open handbag, the revolver pointed right at him. The sight of it jolted him and he forced his glance up while he swallowed and tried to discipline his mind.

20

DONALD TREMAINE had moved one step away from the mantelpiece and there he stopped. Evelyn had leaned forward in the chair, hands on arms, the sudden loss of color in her face the only sign that she was frightened. Standish was still watching the gun, seeing the tip-up action that Ballard had mentioned and knowing now that this was the old Harrington and Richardson model that Ralph Estey had once owned. He started to speak and found he had to swallow first.

"That's Ralph's gun, isn't it? How did you get the other one, the one you used Monday night?"

Sheila Keith was still seated, her weight forward and the wig and dark glasses forgotten. The skin was taut across the high cheekbones now, the small mouth thinly set, the shadowed eyes bright and dangerous.

"Why don't you tell me, Doctor?" she said. "You seem to have all the answers."

Standish found a reasonable assumption, but he took a moment to try to understand this woman. She had fooled him as she had fooled others with her fine figure and bright smile and sexual promise. It was all there if he'd had sense enough to put it together. The background she had given him, the initial drive, the determination, the selfish pursuit of her own goals, even the drama lessons that had better equipped her to play the part. What was it she had said when he had given her a ride the other morning? *You have to learn to be tough. You do what you have to do and never mind who gets hurt.*

Her experience with men needed no comment and he recalled her account of her unhappy marriage. He remembered her matter-of-fact story of how, when she had left her husband, she had stripped the apartment and sold its contents. Estey, or any of his breed, was not enough for her but there was good material in Donald Tremaine. All he needed was money and she had found a way to get it for him.

And Tremaine would not be too suspicious even if he knew of the attention she got from Estey and Flemming. The reason for this, it seemed, lay in the character of the man and the girl's physical appeal, which few could ignore. With Sheila in his arms how could he doubt her? How easy to let her make the decisions, to promise her what she wanted, to wait however long she asked. There had always been women like this and men who danced attendance, but even as Standish understood how it must have been with Tremaine, he found the thought sickening and distasteful.

"All right," he said. "If I have to guess I'll say you didn't have a gun of your own. You needed one to carry out your plan. You knew Flemming had a gun and might even carry one. You already knew what you had to do and he probably jumped at the chance when you said you'd stop at his place for a drink or two. You knew about chloral hydrate and when it worked you cleaned and dried the glasses and put the whiskey away. You found the gun and used it. You didn't forget the paper that contained the drug. You just missed the wastebasket when you threw it away and I happened to get curious about it."

"He was out like a light," she said flatly and with no suggestion of regret in her voice. "Dead to the world. He stayed that way."

"And you kept the gun for Ralph. You had to make the murder-suicide theory stand up. You knew about the fight. You probably couldn't arrange it exactly as it happened but you most certainly did your best to precipitate it. You heard the threat. You heard what Estey said about the gun he had. Had you already made a date with him for a little get-together in the musicians' room before you shot Flemming? Did you suggest that Ralph bring a pint?"

He made himself continue. "That musicians' room was ideal, wasn't it? Ralph had a key to the place. No chance his body would be discovered until the next night. An anonymous call to the police about Flemming. So the time of death could be reasonably established while you were laundering some underwear at your place and washing your hair. And you left Flemming's gun—did Ralph ever see it or did you ease up from behind him and pull the trigger when he wasn't looking? You had to leave that gun, didn't you? Just as you had to take that gun of Ralph's with you."

He hesitated and the enormity of what she had done came back to him. He had to swallow against the sickness inside him, the revulsion in his mind.

"Robert Tremaine I can understand. You didn't know him. You kept it impersonal. He stood between you and what you'd been looking for all your life and a traffic accident to a drunk did not concern you. Flemming became a threat and—"

"Flemming," she interrupted, biting at the words, her mouth a thin red slash, "got just what he'd given to one or two other men. He had it coming. I didn't feel a thing."

"But Estey was your friend. A failure in your eyes maybe—"

"He could have made trouble. He knew some things about me. He was jealous. He would have told Donald. He was a pest and the way he was going he'd have wound up like Jack Teagarden—a better horn man than almost anybody—sick, alone, and dead in some motel room."

She stopped for a second or two. The muscles in her face worked and there was something in her eyes that may have been remorse; then it was gone and her voice was again flat and frigid.

"I didn't want to. Don't you understand? *I had to!*"

Standish let his breath out softly. There it was. As simple as that. In her coldly calculating mind, and having already decided to kill Flemming, she had to kill again. For her there was no other way.

He gave a small unconscious shake of his head to dispel such imagery and now a new thought came to him. "What was the wig for?"

"Because," Tremaine broke in disconsolately, "I have a nosy landlord. Sheila said it wouldn't do for people to know I was in love with her until it was time to get married. She said we ought to keep our affair a secret."

"And why," Standish said, turning to Evelyn, "did you come here last night—and tonight?"

"Because some of the things you told me yesterday scared me. It never occurred to me that Robert's death was anything but an accident but what you said made me begin to wonder." She glanced at Tremaine. "I wanted to know what you told Donald. I came back here tonight because Warren Choate said the police had talked to him late this afternoon about the stock sale last December. I wanted to find out what Donald did with that five thousand dollars in cash."

"You didn't know about Sheila?"

"Not actually." She shook her head determinedly. "I may have suspected that he had a girl—"

"I still don't believe it," Tremaine cut in, his voice heavy and perplexed. "I can't."

"Well, maybe you'll believe this," Standish said, and explained what had happened the previous night. He spoke of the three shots and his prior talk with Sheila. "I guess I scared you too," he said, seeing again the girl's hard bright stare and rigid mouth.

"You knew then that I was crowding Donald. You knew *I* knew he'd been seeing a mysterious brunette regularly. I told you about the chloral hydrate. You even said I was persistent and it worried you plenty. You were afraid when the pressure came that Donald would crack and come to you with his doubts and demand an explanation.

"It had been raining," he said thoughtfully and to no one in particular. "I saw when I got to my feet that the pavement where your car had been was wet. It would have been dry if the car had been there very long. I thought someone"—he looked at Tremaine—"probably you, had followed me to Hennessey's and then on to my apartment."

He glanced at the girl and continued with quiet bitterness. "I couldn't see the obvious answer. You were too good for me. You were the only one who knew where I kept my car. You had a helper in the checkroom—Madge, you said—so you could easily duck out. You got your coat, and the bag with the gun, and stuffed some man's hat under the coat; someone you knew was not about to leave for a while. You told Madge you'd be back in a few minutes. You'd killed twice with Flemming's gun. Why not once more if you could stop me while you still had time?"

Tremaine interrupted again. He seemed not to have been listening and he spoke to Sheila, his bespectacled eyes sick.

"What are you going to do, Sheila?"

"Do?" The girl considered the question, smooth brow wrinkling now and some flick of the eye suggesting that the problem had not yet occurred to her. She glanced at Evelyn and at Standish. She maneuvered the strap of her handbag over her left arm. She draped the coat on top of it and came slowly to her feet. When the wig and dark glasses fell from her lap, she kicked the wig aside and, careful to keep the gun level, stooped to retrieve the glasses.

"I'll tell you," she said finally. "If I thought you were with me, if I was sure I could count on you, I'd take these two"— she waved the gun—"out of here and get rid of them. It could be done. We could get away with it. We could have what we want the rest of our lives."

"I *am* with you, Sheila," Tremaine said, "but not that way. You killed my brother, not yourself but you arranged it—"

"To help you," she said coldly. "To make something out of you. I did you a favor. Before that you were a nothing going nowhere. A two-bit job and no future. You hated him anyway. You said so."

"I know. What you did to Flemming and Estey is done. You have no chance at all unless you try to get away. Maybe I do owe you something. Give me the gun and I'll help you get out of here."

For an instant the narrowed eyes were incredulous. "You must be crazy."

Evelyn Tremaine stood up. When she spoke her voice was forceful and clipped.

"I agree. Let her alone, Donald. Stay out of it."

"No." Tremaine shook his head stubbornly and his jaw was set. "If I'm to blame for some of this I'll take the responsibility, but I want that gun. There's going to be no more killing."

Tremaine took a slow and deliberate step forward and Standish tried to stop him. "Don't be a fool!" he said.

Tremaine did not seem to hear. He had eyes only for the girl and when his chin came up he seemed to stretch taller, his face gray and traces of shock beginning to show through. He was still ten feet away but he had his hand out.

"Give it to me, Sheila. It's the only way. I said I'd help, and I will."

"No!"

She stiffened and the gun, which had been pointed at Standish, shifted to Tremaine. She watched him take another careful step and now the mouth flattened and the green eyes had a wild and glassy look that was no longer quite sane.

"No. I'm getting out of here."

"Donald!" It was Evelyn Tremaine and her voice was ragged. "Let her go."

"Yes," Tremaine said. "But not with that gun. I mean it, Sheila."

And suddenly the tension that had been working on Standish wound tightly inside him and a chill ran up his spine.

He knew somehow that the girl would never surrender the gun. To her Tremaine remained a threat and she was no longer rational. She said as much in the next instant. She tried to back up but a table got in her way. She seemed to brace herself, half screaming now, threatening him because she seemed aware, as Standish was, that Tremaine had somehow set a goal for himself and had no intention of stopping.

Standish felt his scalp tighten and the perspiration was drying coldly on his spine. He added his warning to Evelyn's, not knowing what he said but trying to get Tremaine's attention. He was on his feet now, beside the arm of the divan, and as he glanced round he saw the pillow. He started to reach for it surreptitiously even as he shouted a final warning. He saw Tremaine keep moving, hands still outstretched, saw the trigger finger tighten as he recognized the brutal resolution that filmed the girl's bright and desperate gaze.

He had one corner of the pillow in his fingers, knowing there was no more time, and at the same instant the knock came at the door, sounding loud and imperative, a shocking sound in the otherwise quiet room. It startled everyone and for one brief moment all movement ceased.

Sheila's hand remained tight on the revolver but her head turned a fraction of an inch, her attention momentarily distracted. It was then that Standish spun the pillow toward the girl's face and tried to follow it. He heard the first shot and then, so quickly that it must have been a reflex that yanked the trigger, the second.

This shot, he knew, had hit the pillow. It seemed to jump in mid-air; then hang there. Before it fell he was on top of the girl, one arm clamping around her waist, the other twisting the hot gun from her hand.

For a few frantic seconds she fought with him, wildly and without purpose. He half lifted her toward the chair, crushing her taut straining body to him, thrusting his hip into her stomach to keep her from kneeing him. He put the gun on the table to free his other hand and then, surprisingly, a sudden spasm seemed to hit her. Her body went slack and he had to support her for another step before he could lower her into the chair.

He was breathing hard now, emotions still shaken as he turned to find Tremaine looking down at the small but spreading stain on the left arm of his sport shirt. This told him where the first shot had gone and now the knocking came again more insistently. Evelyn Tremaine, who had been standing white-faced and rigid, reacted first. With a quick breath and a resolute toss of her head, she strode over to open the door.

Standish, watching her and half expecting Lieutenant Ballard, stared incredulously as Mary Hayward moved slowly across the threshold. He saw the wide-open gray eyes slide swiftly round the room and the trembling of her lower lip before she started toward him.

"Paul," she breathed. "Are you all right?" And then the words came tumbling out. "The lieutenant wasn't in. They said he'd be back soon, that they would give him the message. I tried to be patient. I wanted to wait but it seemed as if you were up here forever. I got scared. I had to come. I had to know—"

She ran out of breath and left the sentence dangling. Standish helped her.

"It's all right, Mary," he said, his initial astonishment giving way to a curious feeling of warmth and pride and understanding. "It's probably a good thing you knocked. We're okay now—except for Mr. Tremaine. If you'll go down and get my bag, we'll patch him up."

"*Donald!*"

Again it was the shocked and startled voice of Evelyn Tremaine. Something in its cadence made Standish wheel and then he knew why. For Tremaine, unnoticed until now, had picked up the revolver Standish had discarded. He held it in his good right hand and moved the muzzle up.

Standish, with no further capacity for amazement, simply peered at the man. He tried to find some answer in the tired eyes and failed. After that anger asserted itself.

"What the hell's the matter with you?" he demanded. "What do you think you're going to do with that?"

"Nothing, I hope. . . . Sheila! Listen to me!"

There was new authority in the tone and the girl lifted her head. Her cheeks were slack and colorless in that moment. The green eyes were stunned and uncomprehending, but he succeeded in getting her attention.

"I said I'd help you, and I will. How much money do you have?"

She still did not understand. She had to wet her lips and swallow. She fumbled ineffectively with her handbag.

"I—I don't know, Donald. With me do you mean? Not much."

"At home."

"Maybe four hundred in the dresser drawer."

Tremaine pointed with the gun toward the kneehole desk in the corner. "Go over there. Open the top left-hand drawer. In the back. There's an envelope." He watched her rise and start uncertainly toward the desk. "I like to keep some cash on hand," he said to no one in particular.

Standish realized now what Tremaine had in mind but he still did not understand it. He saw the girl locate the envelope. He watched her take out the fifty-dollar bills when Tremaine said: "Count it."

"Eight hundred," she said, her voice still full of wonder.

"With your four that's twelve. Take it. Pack a small bag when you pick up your money. I can probably give you an hour's head start. He glanced from face to face, eyes strangely steady and his words sardonic. "I don't think the girls will bother me, and Standish—he's a reasonable man, aren't you, Doctor? You're no cop. You have no authority, no obligation, no duty to perform—not at the risk of a bullet in the leg. As for this"—he looked at the blood stain on his sleeve, which had not spread very much—"I don't think I'll bleed to death in an hour."

Again it was Evelyn Tremaine who found words before the others. "You're going to help her get away?" she said in sharp astonishment. "For God's sake why?"

"It will make you an accessory," Standish said.

"Not to murder. I don't know what the penalty is for helping a suspect escape but I'm willing to risk it."

Evelyn tried again. "But don't you know what she's like now? Don't you realize what she's done?"

"Yes. I'm not condoning what she did. I'm sick to death of the thought that she could be so cold and calculating and inhuman. I feel like throwing up. I probably will when this is over. . . . Why?" he added, coming now to his sister-in-law's original question. "Maybe because I was in love with her for a while. Maybe because she made me feel I was someone for the first time in my life. Maybe I don't even have a reason but I do know she's the only woman who ever made me feel important, who made me feel like a man. I owe her something for that. . . . Get going, Sheila!"

There was no further protest. It was as if the others were still under the influence of some lingering spell that only time could eradicate. Standish offered no argument because he knew it would be futile. He also began to get some understanding of what was in Tremaine's mind. That he was, perhaps, somewhat irrational on his stand and that he would eventually realize this, was no longer important. He had given his reasons and right now they were sufficient unto him.

Standish could see as the girl started to back toward the door that new color was showing in her cheeks. Some of the confidence was back and the green eyes were again calculating and watchful. She reached behind her to turn the knob. She started to say something, stopped, tried again.

"Thanks, Donald. I'm sorry I hurt you."

"It isn't important," Tremaine said, his voice sounding flat, tired, and spent. "You probably won't make it—and I'm not sure I care—but you've got an hour to give it a try."

She was gone then and for a few seconds the room was still. Tremaine moved to a straight-backed chair and sat down so he could watch the three of them. The palms of Standish's hands were still damp and when he brought out a handkerchief to dry them he could feel the strain beginning to ease in his neck and shoulders. As he reached for cigarettes he asked Tremaine about the arm.

"It'll do," the man said. He was holding it up now, the fingers shoulder-high. "It must have missed the bone."

"If it hadn't you wouldn't be moving it," Standish said, and was about to continue when he heard the sudden sound of commotion somewhere outside and below the room. For another second or so he did not know what caused it. Then he heard the muffled sound of a woman's voice, high-pitched and furiously complaining. It seemed to come from the hallway and the floor below.

Tremaine had already jumped to his feet, the bespectacled eyes darting from side to side in quick alarm. "What's that?" he said sharply.

The sounds were closer now, on the stairs it seemed. The woman was complaining in the same furious voice but now there were other voices, not distinct as yet but definitely male.

Standish thought he knew the answer this time. He took a small breath and let it out, certain now that Ballard had at last responded to Mary Hayward's telephone message. For the first time it began to dawn on him that Tremaine's stubborn and foolhardy effort to get the gun from Sheila Keith so she could not use it again had been worthwhile after all. He was already at the door when the knock came. He saw the still struggling girl firmly supported between Lieutenant Ballard and Sergeant Cooney, and like that, half dragging and half carrying her, they entered the room.

It was nearly two o'clock before matters were in hand and preliminary statements taken. The State's Attorney had been consulted and it was agreed that the formal statements could wait until morning. Donald Tremaine's wound had been a minor one, as he had suspected, and there was no charge against him pending further investigation. Finally only Standish and Mary were left in Ballard's office as the lieutenant went over and closed the door. He found a half-filled bottle of whiskey in the lower drawer and brought out paper cups.

"This," he said happily, "is strictly against regulations." He poured a spot of whiskey in each cup, added water from the cooler. "No ice," he said, and then sat down, saluted with his cup, and drank gratefully.

"Well," he said, when he had a cigarette going, "I hate to admit it, and I was a long time seeing it your way, but you were right again, Doc."

"So were you."

"Hunh?"

"About the chloral hydrate." Standish smiled. "Almost from the first you said if anyone had fed it to Flemming it was the girl. And she did."

"Yeah. . . . That's right, I did." Ballard chuckled at the memory and then said: "When did you really tumble it was her?"

"Not until this afternoon when I got word from Clem Jones and found out Sheila was the mysterious brunette who had been seeing Tremaine Sunday or Monday nights— the only ones she was free. After that things began to add up pretty fast."

"But what did Clem have to do with it?"

"He analyzed some hair for me." He explained about the black hair he had found in Donald Tremaine's apartment and what he had done with it. "Clem said it was dyed."

"So?"

"Dyed all the way. From tip to tip." Standish sampled

his drink and it tasted good. "As a matter of fact, it wasn't even human hair. Some synthetic they've been using recently since the wig business started to get big."

"Oh." Ballard nodded. "Yeah," he said. "And a brunette like Mrs. Tremaine would hardly be wearing a brunette wig. . . . And the hell of it is—excuse me, Mary—she would have gotten away with it if you hadn't found that little 'powder paper' she discarded and then had it tested for chloral hydrate. . . . What would the chances be of finding traces of the drug in Flemming when you did the p.m. if you hadn't already suspected it?"

"Remote."

"Yeah." Ballard grinned, his eyes friendly and respectful. "You're like old Doc Lathrop," he said. "You got curious and you didn't care what anybody said, or if it was your business or not, you couldn't let it go until you had the truth. I guess that was it, hunh?"

Standish tried to consider the question objectively. He was too tired to feel any sense of personal accomplishment but he did remember Ralph Estey's insurance policy that would now be paid to his young son and the thought that he had been able to clear his friend's name was strangely satisfying. He did not say so. He did not want to talk about it. It seemed much easier to agree with Ballard.

"Maybe something like that, Tom," he said finally. But even as he spoke he remembered Sheila's strange appeal and it came to him that, given a different set of circumstances, he might have been no more able to resist her than Donald Tremaine and the others.

It was not a flattering thought, or an easy one to dismiss. He finished his drink and stood up, and Mary was beside him as he said good night to Ballard and took her arm. It felt firm and warm under his hand, and as she smiled up at him he knew that here at least was something real, something honest, something good.